Part One

Tornado

1

Aunt Tuula

The cold wind that whipped snow through the canyons of New York's city streets matched my mood as I hurried back to Aunt Tuula's apartment on Friday afternoon. My first soccer practice at the Girls' International School of Manhattan had not gone well—to put it bluntly, it was awful.

I had let myself, and my old team, down. Of course, the Golden Bears were four thousand miles away in Finland and would never know I'd played terribly unless I e-mailed to tell them, which I was *not* going to do. Instead, I vowed to practice harder and play better. Then when I *did* talk to my friends back home, I'd be able to tell them that I had showed these New Yorkers what a Golden Bear could do!

Satisfied with that thought, I pulled my blue woolen scarf over my mouth and leaned into the wind. I was undaunted by the frigid force because it reminded me of the northern country I'd left behind. It also made me more comfortable with my new life in the United States.

My older sister and I had been living with our aunt Tuula in her Manhattan apartment less than a month. After my mother had died, it was what my father and Aunt Tuula had thought best. Even though it was hard to leave behind everything I knew, it was exciting, and I was happy to be around kids who wouldn't feel sorry for me all the time because of my mother.

Rona had settled into city life easily; she was thrilled to be able to study ballet and modern dance with world-famous teachers. For her, the heavy work schedule was the perfect distraction from our mother's sudden death six months ago, and it was all she talked about the few moments we had together, which was fine with me. I didn't know what we could say to each other that would help.

I had hoped soccer would help me escape, like Rona's dancing did for her, but I was used to playing outside on a grassy field or in the thawing slush of early spring, and I was used to being one of the best players. I am not good at everything, but I am almost always good at sports. But here, in the indoor gym, I couldn't get into the rhythm during drills, and it made me remember my mother. She had always softened my disappointments as no one else could. She made me feel better without making me feel like I should be different.

Except for that, my first week at GIS had gone better than I dared hope, thanks mostly to my new friend Birdie Cramer Bright. We are not at all alike. Birdie is dreamy, and I like plans. Birdie loves to talk about plants, and I like to take hikes. Birdie is usually shy and careful with what she says, and I am comfortable with people and too outspoken for some. But even though we're very different, our friendship really works, and that's all that matters.

Birdie had just moved to New York from California, and this had been her first week at GIS, too. We had both been too busy adjusting to a new city and school to talk about our journey in Aventurine, which had happened just before New Year's. Birdie had promised to come by, and I wished she would visit soon. We also had something in common that we couldn't discuss with anyone else: generations of women in our families had been trained and guided by fairies in the dreamland of Aventurine to become fairy godmothers.

Thinking of Birdie and Aventurine lightened my mood. As the howl and bite of the wind diminished, I imagined myself walking through miles of orchards, riding the Redbird Wind, and battling deadly vines. I'm not a daydreamer like Birdie, so my thoughts about the fantastic world weren't made up, I promise you. They were real memories. I had been sleeping with my Kalis stick under my pillow all week, waiting for the fairies to take me back to Aventurine.

"Good afternoon, Miss Laine." Mr. Bender, the doorman of my aunt's apartment building, nodded slightly. Tall with snow white hair, he looked like royalty in his blue uniform trimmed in gold. His friendly greeting was real, and he smiled with his eyes.

"Hello, Mr. Bender." I pulled my scarf down and smiled back, an exchange of mutual respect. "Just call me Kerka." I said this every day.

"Miss Kerka it is." Mr. Bender winked and held the door open, which he did every day as well.

I dashed inside and ran to the elevator, despite my aunt's warnings that other residents might not approve. Since running covered more ground in fewer steps and less time, I figured old people didn't *like* it because they couldn't *do* it. Which hardly seemed fair. At that time, however, no one else was in the lobby, and Mr. Bender, unlike Aunt Tuula, didn't care.

As I rode alone in the elevator, my thoughts rebelled and flashed back to my bad soccer playing. If I didn't get better soon, I would have no chance of being chosen as the GIS starting forward during spring tryouts.

I unlocked the door and burst into my aunt's huge apartment. I didn't mean to slam the door behind me; I just pushed it too hard. The noise boomed through the sparsely furnished rooms, shaking the walls and jingling the wind chimes hanging in the tall front window.

"You're just in time, Kerka!" Aunt Tuula called out cheerfully from the kitchen. "I'll have a nice, hot treat ready as soon as you change."

"Okay, Aunt Tuula!" I called back. A wall separated the kitchen from the living room and entrance hall. My aunt couldn't see into the foyer, but it was no mystery how she knew that I had come in and not my sister. Rona was *always* at ballet rehearsal, and when she was in the apartment, she floated about like the gentlest breeze.

Here's a little bit about Rona. She is two years

older than me, fifteen, nearly sixteen. She is quiet, graceful, and an extraordinary dancer. She would never slam a door, even by accident.

Aunt Tuula stepped into the kitchen doorway as I dropped my backpack and took off my scarf. In her forties and slim, she was almost always smiling. Her sandy blond hair was so long she could sit on her braids. Except on those days when she washed her hair, she twined the braids up and around her head like a crown and used wire hairpins to hold them in place. All the women in my family wore their hair in braids one way or another. Braids are good at keeping your hair out of your face so you can see what you're doing.

"You always enter a room like a tempest, Kerka," Aunt Tuula said. Holding a small mixing bowl, she leaned against the doorjamb and continued stirring. "How was your day?"

"I scored a hundred percent on the pop quiz in math, and no one gave too much homework, so school was fine." I shrugged out of my parka and sighed. "But soccer practice was a disaster. A gym is too small for soccer drills; I wish we could play outside."

"You'll get used to it," Aunt Tuula said gently,

"and then your star will shine again. You don't like the challenge?"

"I don't mind having to work hard, but I hate having to work hard at something I've already worked hard at and should be good at," I explained.

Aunt Tuula held up the spoon and tipped it so that white icing spilled off in a ribbon of milky ooze. Then she deftly switched topics from awful soccer to awesome pastry. "I'm making hot cross buns. They're just what you need to take the chill off."

"They smell great!" I inhaled the aroma of dough heating in the oven. "I'll hurry and change out of my uniform."

"Excellent. Then we can have a nice, long talk. I haven't forgotten my promise." Aunt Tuula's merry smile shifted slightly. "Rona won't be home until quite late again." As she swept back into the kitchen, the wind chimes jingled again.

Since our arrival in New York ten days before Christmas, it seemed as though Rona and I had taken two different paths that hardly ever crossed. Rona left before I woke up every morning and often didn't return until I was in the middle of homework or asleep. The ballet company was in rehearsal for a new production, and Rona had a major role. I didn't know what it was. I hadn't had a chance to ask. I realized that we hadn't said more than ten words to each other since last Sunday.

But that's nine words more than Biba's said in the past six months, I thought as I opened the coat closet in the foyer.

My separation from Rona started almost immediately after our mother was in the car accident. One day Aiti—that's *Mom* in Finnish—was there, and then she was gone. Our youngest sister, Biba, stopped speaking altogether. No one knows what that means, but Aunt Tuula and my father decided that Biba should stay in Finland with him. All four of my grandparents still lived in our village, so he would have them to help with Biba, too.

Biba's silence and Rona's busyness bothered me more than I let my father know. I knew that eventually it would change, and I didn't want to have to talk and talk about it to "make me feel better." Thankfully, Aunt Tuula seemed to understand. She didn't try to make me talk about my feelings. But even without talking about it, the feeling of something missing was always there, like a thundercloud that followed me around.

After stuffing my scarf and mittens in the sleeves, I hung my parka on a hanger in the closet and kicked off my boots. They hit the back wall with a thud. I took my Kalis stick out of my backpack and left the backpack on the closet floor. A year ago, my mother had given a stick to each of us—Biba, Rona, and me. Mine was twelve inches long, with a delicately carved *D* in the wood. It was my most prized possession, and I kept it with me at all times, although it was not always in my hand. The stick stayed inside my backpack when I was at school.

I kicked the door closed and winced when it slammed. In the kitchen, Aunt Tuula laughed. She sounded like my mother.

I paused before turning down the hall. I tossed my orange Kalis stick from one hand to the other as I scanned the large, sunlit living room. The spacious apartment, with its high ceilings, ornate woodwork, and bare hardwood floors, was pleasant but still didn't quite feel like home. A large, boxy sofa, two matching chairs, and a square coffee table by one window were the only furniture in the front room. My mother had stuffed our house in Finland full of both practical necessities and whimsical treasures. I closed my eyes to picture it more clearly.

Tapestries woven with images of magical creatures hung on the walls. Even in my mind, the unicorns, elves, gargoyles, and fairies watched my every move. When I was younger, I was sure they told my mother every tiny naughty thing I did. Thick rugs, each woven with a design inspired by nature, covered the flat stone and tiled floors. Family photographs and painted portraits graced the fireplace mantels and staircase walls.

The memory made me both happy and sad. Nothing could bring my mother or my old life back, but there were things in my new life to love, especially my aunt, with her odd quirks and lifestyle.

Aunt Tuula had a reason for her lack of furnishings. She had explained to me that she didn't want the art and artifacts she had brought back from her world travels as a translator for the U.N. to have to compete for attention with mundane clutter. Almost every continent was represented in her apartment: there were jade animals from China, masks and drums from Africa, boomerangs from Australia, and fine crystal from Europe. South American baskets sat on top of the kitchen cabinets. Turkish mosaics, Japanese scrolls, and old American tintype photographs hung on the walls among carved animals, beaded jewelry, and ancient cooking utensils.

I hurried into my room, which Aunt Tuula had furnished more like my room in Finland. Although far from cluttered, my little haven felt nicely full with a chest of drawers, a desk and chair, a rocker, a large bed with a carved headboard, and three reading lamps. The smoky-blue bedspread had a flower-and-vine border that looked like the designs on our carpets at home and now reminded me of Queen Patchouli's fairy circle in Aventurine.

Dropping my Kalis stick on the bed, I pulled off my school uniform and changed into jeans, a sweater, and heavy socks. As I dropped my school clothes in my hamper, my eye was drawn to my second-most prized possession, a framed photograph of my mother and Aunt Tuula when they were teenagers. I picked up the picture. Smiling, with their braided hair pinned in buns over their ears like blond Princess Leias, Aiti and Tuula held the large trophy they had won in a folk dance competition. Aiti had promised to teach my sisters and me the traditional Scandinavian dances she had performed—but not until we had mastered the more important Kalis dance.

Before my mother died, she had started teaching my sisters and me the basic steps of the Kalis dance. She had dropped hints that we would carry on the traditions of our fairy godmother heritage, the Pax Lineage, but she said only enough to tease my curiosity. I set down the photo and picked up the Kalis stick. Aunt Tuula had promised on her heart's honor to explain these mysteries to me when I turned thirteen. My thirteenth birthday was the next day.

Grabbing my Kalis stick, I dashed out the bedroom door, but I didn't run down the hallway. I jumped and twirled, performing the two Kalis dance moves that lifted my spirits. My mother called them the Wind Leap and the Tornado Spin.

Launching off the balls of my feet, I bounded into the air. I stretched to lengthen the arc, and pushed off again when I landed. My spring-power had grown over the past few months, and now I went high enough to graze the ceiling with my stick. Clearing the hall in three long leaps, I began to spin the instant my toes touched the living room floor.

I jumped, twisting my body in the air. Then, mimicking a tornado's erratic skips across the landscape, I performed a series of fast twirls across the floor, shifting from one foot to the other as I turned. Leap and spin, twirl — one, two, three — leap! I felt like I was flying, and with each spin I shed a layer of the stress and sorrow that had darkened my day.

The wind chimes jangled as I whizzed past in a dizzying finale, and the world looked a little brighter when I came to

an abrupt halt in the kitchen doorway. I had to remember that even if soccer didn't go well, my Kalis
dancing was still good—and that was what mattered
the most!

2

Cider and Hot Cross Buns

Aunt Tuula's kitchen was my second-favorite room in the apartment, after my bedroom. A self-taught chef, Aunt Tuula was equipped for gourmet cooking, and she was always trying out new recipes from the countries she had visited. Crystal and china were stored in cabinets with glass-pane doors. Above a butcher-block island, a suspended rack held gleaming pots and pans, dried herbs tied with twine, and a variety of ladles and spatulas and utensils I didn't know the names of. A bright orange towel hung on a hook, and several salt-and-pepper shakers—all shaped like gargoyles—looked down from a shelf above the stove. Beside them, an elf figurine sat on a red-maple-leaf dish.

A pan of cooling buns rested on an iron trivet by the gargoyle sugar bowl and the elf. Another pan cooled on the stove. The fresh buns filled the room with a delicious aroma, and my teeth ached to bite into them.

"That was dazzling, Kerka!" Aunt Tuula exclaimed. She stood between the stove and the island, holding an icing dispenser.

"Thank you." I beamed with pride as I perched on a stool. The Kalis dance was the *only* dance I was better at than Rona, probably because it required as much speed and power as it did grace.

"You've been practicing." Aunt Tuula finished spooning icing into the dispenser tube and capped it with a nozzle.

"Every day," I said. I didn't tell Aunt Tuula that I wanted to be the best Kalis dancer ever in the Pax Lineage of fairy godmothers.

"It makes up for soccer a little," I added. "Still, I'll need to work on the soccer drills inside on my own. Maybe I'll stay after practice next week."

"That would probably help." Upending the icing tube, Aunt Tuula pushed the plunger and drew icing crosses on top of the buns. "Just don't practice in the living room."

I laughed out loud. I imagined a soccer ball bombing one of her antiques, then rebounding off the walls from one rare object to another until nothing was left but piles of broken glass, bent metal, and splintered wood.

"No soccer practice in the living room," I said, faking a gravely serious face and placing my hand over my heart.

"Thank you." Aunt Tuula's eyes twinkled as she turned to stir a pot of cider heating on the stove. "I may have another, less destructive solution."

"What?" I asked, growing serious for real. "Is there an indoor soccer field in New York?"

"No, but there's a handball court in the basement of this building," Aunt Tuula explained. "I'm sure we can use it in the afternoon, when most of the resident handball players are at work or taking their children to piano lessons or having afternoon tea at the café."

"That would be great! I'll practice at midnight if I have to!" I said.

"Hopefully it will not come to that," Aunt Tuula replied. She took a sip of cider, savored the flavor, and frowned. "Almost, but not quite right," she muttered. Setting the wooden spoon on a shiny silver spoon rest, she opened a bag of spices and added a few pinches to the steaming pot.

"There's almost nothing better than hot spiced cider on a cold January day," Aunt Tuula said as she continued stirring.

"What *is* better?" I asked.

"Hot chocolate with nutmeg and marshmallows, or French vanilla tea with sugar and cream," Aunt Tuula replied. She looked at me over her shoulder with an impish grin. "It depends on the day or the mood or both."

"Why is today a hot-cider day?" I was genuinely curious and very interested.

"Because hot cider with cinnamon tastes wonderful with warm hot cross buns," Aunt Tuula said. "A famous chef in Paris gave me this recipe. He told me I was the only person he had ever given the recipe to."

The individual mounds of dough had fused together during baking. Using a spatula, Aunt Tuula separated a square bun from the others in the pan, lifted it out, and put it on a plate, which she handed to me.

I bit into the warm bread. "This is incredible!"

Grinning, Aunt Tuula sampled a bun and nodded with approval. "Perfect! I'm so pleased when my creations turn out right. They don't always."

She lifted out a third bun and put it on the maple-leaf dish.

There was no need for a third plate unless we were expecting a third person. "Is Rona coming home early after all?" I asked.

"No, I'm afraid not." Aunt Tuula sighed. I could tell she was both happy and sad about my sister's success with the ballet, like me.

I frowned, puzzled. "Then who gets the third bun?"

"The kitchen elf," Aunt Tuula answered. "You should know from Britta that it's wise to stay on good terms with elves. They can be such stinkers when they think they've been wronged."

Britta was my mother's name. "Of course, Aiti told us," I agreed. "But it was just a part of the sto ries; I didn't know that elves were still here, in the waking world."

My sisters and I had fallen asleep many nights listening to my parents tell us folktales. Many of the stories were about elves. Guardians of their homes, elves bring good fortune and health to the people who live or work within the same walls, but only if the elves are treated with respect. Disaster befalls anyone who fails to repay an elf's favor or takes an elf's gifts for granted. Santa Claus, the most famous elf of all time, is a perfect example. Children think he won't bring presents if they're naughty. My father said that Santa rarely withheld gifts, and then only in the worst cases.

"I've never seen an elf here myself, but I know they are around," Aunt Tuula went on. "They stick to themselves for the most part, even in Aventurine, but your great-great-grandmother Elsa met an elf. She said he was quite unpleasant."

"Why was he unpleasant?" I asked.

"Well, the story goes that Elsa had a terrible fight with her sister, Marjo," Aunt Tuula explained. "They stayed angry for so long, Elsa couldn't remember why they had argued, but it was over something silly—like missing socks. The elf demanded that Elsa conduct herself as a proper member of the Pax Lineage and make peace with Marjo so he could get some sleep."

I mulled that over for a moment, then asked, "Why couldn't the elf sleep?"

Aunt Tuula paused to look me in the eye. "It is said that our family's destinies and the fate of elves are intertwined."

"Seriously?" I asked.

Aunt Tuula chuckled. "It's what my aiti always

said. The theory has never been proved, but it hasn't been disproved, either."

"If Grandmother believed it, then I do, too," I said.

"You'll have an elf in your kitchen someday, whether you can see it or not. We all do," Aunt Tuula added. "They prefer kitchens."

I nodded. "That's where the goodies are," I said, taking another bite of my bun.

"That's it exactly." Aunt Tuula cast a fond glance at the elf figurine on the leaf. "I suspect *this* little guy comes to life and snitches treats and makes tea at night when no one is up and about to see."

I sat up straighter. "Is that why Aiti never washed the dessert plates until morning? So the elf in the kitchen tapestry could have the crumbs and the pieces Rona never finished?"

"That or she was just tired from being a mother of three energetic girls." Aunt Tuula pulled a yellow sunflower pot holder off a hook. "Britta bought the tapestry that hangs in your living room when she was twenty, shortly after we became fairy godmothers. It always looked to me as if it had been woven in Aventurine, or at least by someone who had been there."

I nodded. Over the years, I had spent hours staring at the woven picture of the elf sleeping under a toadstool surrounded by ladybugs, butterflies, flowers, and ferns. I was constantly spotting tiny things I hadn't seen before. I wondered if anyone was leaving cake and cookie crumbs for the elf now that my mother was gone. Maybe when my grandmother came over, she would tell Biba.

I changed the subject. "Where did Great-Great-Grandmother Elsa meet the elf?"

"In Aventurine," Aunt Tuula said as she brushed crumbs off the countertop.

My aunt's reluctance to talk about the fairy world had been as frustrating as my messing up in soccer practice. Now that the topic had been broached, I quickly asked another question.

"Did *you* go to Aventurine?" I nibbled the last piece of my hot cross bun.

"Of course," Aunt Tuula admitted. "Every girl from a fairy godmother lineage goes to Aventurine at least once when she's young, and a few go many times. It's where we learn our craft and gain the wisdom to do our jobs."

"Do you ever go back to visit once you are a full-fledged fairy godmother?"

"No, never," Aunt Tuula said with a shake of her head. "Grown-ups cannot go except under very special circumstances."

"What kind of special circumstances?" I couldn't stand the thought of never seeing fairies again or of being barred from their lands. I hadn't had an amazing adventure of my own yet or learned enough about magic.

"The thing about very special circumstances, Kerka," Aunt Tuula explained, "is that you don't know they're very special circumstances until they happen."

"I hope they happen to me a lot," I said.

Aunt Tuula sensed my dismay. "It doesn't seem like it now, perhaps, but you won't miss Aventurine as much when you're grown up." She paused, sipping her cider and staring past me with a faraway look.

Shaking off the moment, Aunt Tuula continued. "Our lives progress through a series of phases, and we're usually ready to leave the old phase behind when it's time to move on to the next."

"Like when *I* become a fairy godmother?" I asked.

"Yes, like that." Aunt Tuula wrapped the pot holder around the handle of the cider pot. Gripping the handle with two hands, she carefully poured the hot amber liquid into two mugs. "But before you can be a fairy godmother, you have to be a fairy-godmother-in-the-making."

I paid attention to my aunt, but Queen Patchouli had told Birdie and me the same thing the week before.

"The fairies in Aventurine teach fairy-godmothers-in-the-making everything they need to know to use their gifts for good in the real world." Aunt Tuula dropped a cinnamon stick into each mug. "But not every girl who enters Aventurine becomes a fairy godmother."

I knew that girls could fail. Queen Patchouli had warned Birdie that her future as a fairy godmother depended on the outcome of her quest. And Birdie's mom had given up trying to be a fairy godmother when she was only a little older than us. I remembered the Willowood fairy queen's words: *"There are things you have to learn to become a fairy godmother. Things about yourself, other people, the way the world can be changed."*

Aunt Tuula handed me a mug. "With Britta gone, I'm the only full fairy godmother in our branch of the Pax Lineage, and so I'll remain until someone from your generation completes a quest in Aventurine."

"Who?" I asked. "When?"

"Britta wanted you and your sisters to learn the lessons of the Pax Lineage together," Aunt Tuula went on. "However, since Biba is so much younger, the beginning of your training was delayed."

"We learned our first Kalis dance move just over a year ago," I said, "when Biba turned seven."

"You and your sisters have done extremely well, considering," Aunt Tuula said with a sad smile. "But all you have are the most basic dance moves."

A shiver shot up my spine. "What do you mean?"

"Come into the living room, where it's more comfortable." Without further comment, Aunt Tuula picked up her mug and walked out of the warm kitchen.

I followed with my Kalis stick in one hand and my mug in the other. I had done okay, even well, when I was with Birdie in Aventurine, but it had not been my quest. Was I somehow not prepared for my own mission in Aventurine? Birdie was from the Arbor Lineage, and her green magic was so strong that she had traveled to Aventurine with only half of

the Singing Stone, the talisman that helped
her family's girls get to Aventurine in
their dreams. Birdie knew the names
of a million plants and spoke Latin, so
she had been, in some ways, prepared
for what happened in Aventurine.

Powerful gusts shook the window panes in the
living room and seeped through the smallest cracks.
Aunt Tuula set her mug on the coffee table and began
pulling the curtains against the draft. Slipping my
Kalis stick under a large throw pillow, I snuggled
under the Scottish plaid blanket on the sofa, as I
waited for Aunt Tuula to speak. I held my mug in
both hands to warm them. I hadn't told Aunt Tuula
that I had been to Aventurine already, because . . . well, I wasn't sure why; it just wasn't something I wanted to talk about with anyone but Birdie.
I wondered if I should have said something, and if it
was too late to speak now.

"There, that's better." Aunt Tuula sank into one
of the chairs and picked up her mug.

"Will *you* help me with my Kalis training, Aunt
Tuula?" I couldn't hold back any longer, and I didn't
give her time to answer but plunged ahead, making
my case. "Aiti died before she taught us the last basic
Kalis dance move. I know it's the hardest, and I want

to make sure I learn it correctly. I promise that I'll work hard and practice every day, even if I have to give up soccer."

"I have no doubt," Aunt Tuula said. "Your determination to survive and succeed will serve you well in the challenges that lie ahead."

I shifted uneasily and set my mug on the coffee table. The words of praise had an undertone of something not quite right.

"But you are still underprepared." Aunt Tuula rested her elbows on her knees. She suddenly seemed worried to me. "Turning thirteen is a big step for every girl, the moment when she crosses the threshold between childhood and early womanhood."

This was not what I wanted to hear. I knew I couldn't stop time, but I was determined to put off growing up as long as possible.

"When Rona turned thirteen, your mother told her more about our family and our special heritage." Aunt Tuula paused again to clear a catch in her throat. "Britta told me years ago that if anything happened to her, I was to tell you the same things on the eve of your thirteenth birthday."

"That's today." I had to catch my lip in my teeth to keep it from trembling.

"Yes, it is," Aunt Tuula said gently. "Listen,

Kerka. The things your ancestors learned can guide you through the trials that lie ahead. I already told you about Great-Great-Grandmother Elsa and the elf. But there is more to know."

I put my head on the large sofa pillow and fell asleep to the soothing sound of my aunt's voice, holding on to my Kalis stick.

Part Two

Hurricane

3

Into Aventurine

I didn't want to wake up, but the ground was hard despite the dry leaves.

Leaves?

My eyes snapped open. The light was dim, and I was lying in a forest clearing, staring into the soft brown eyes of a squirrel. *Where am I?* I thought for all of two seconds before I knew the answer: I was back in Aventurine!

The squirrel sat on its haunches, chewing a nut and staring back at me.

"Hello," I said to the squirrel. I didn't remember ever seeing a squirrel the last time I was here.

The squirrel scampered away when I sat up. I looked around and quickly recognized where I was: the center of the Willowood, where the Willowood Fairies live. The circular clearing in the middle of the willow trees was filled with mist, and a soft light was coming from one side, as if the sun was just rising. Last time, Birdie and I had all sorts of crazy adventures just trying to reach the Willowood. Already being here had to be a good thing. The queen of the Willowood Fairies could tell me what my mission was, and I could get started right away.

I stood up to start looking for Queen Patchouli or any of the fairies, and I noticed my backpack on the ground. Last time I came, a special map was in my backpack when I arrived. I picked up my backpack and opened it. Except for my orange Kalis stick, which was tucked inside, the canvas bag was empty: no schoolbooks and no map tied with red string.

I'm not sure how Zally's magical map came to be in my backpack when I met Birdie, but I hoped it would show up if I needed it again. I had no doubt that I *would* need it. Zally, a girl around our age who drew the map and sent messages in explosions of sparks, had told us that the geography of Aventurine changes with every dream and every dreamer.

"Good morning!" The voice was a familiar one.

The mist cleared to make a path down the middle of the clearing, and I could see Queen Patchouli on the far side. She was standing in front of what looked like two giant toadstools while a pair of fairies built a fire beside her. "Come, Kerka!" she called.

I looked down to brush dirt off my jeans. But I was no longer wearing jeans! Instead, bits of leaves and moss stuck to a long navy T-shirt with a golden bear on it, long navy shorts, white kneesocks, and cleats. It was the soccer uniform that I wore in Finland—maybe that's what I had been about to dream of before I was pulled into Aventurine! I smiled, thinking, *I'll have to tell Birdie about this.*

Then I really smiled when I remembered another cool thing about Aventurine. There was no need to brush dirt off myself—Queen Patchouli would give me clothes to fit whatever journey I was about to go on!

I shook leaves and dirt off the blue mountains and yellow stags that were embroidered on my backpack and slung the bag over my shoulder. As I headed across the clearing, I watched where I put my feet. Squirrels, chipmunks, rabbits, and mice seemed to be having their breakfasts in the clearing. It was interesting: when Birdie and I were here, everything was covered with flowers; now there were as many small woodland animals as there were plants.

As I drew closer, I heard the buzzing of the bees that often circled Queen Patchouli. A net of morning mist swirled about her flowing emerald gown, and sprinkles of starlight shone in her long hair. A shimmer of green was reflected in her huge iridescent blue wings, which opened and closed like a butterfly's. Long wind-chime earrings made a pure but quiet sound when she moved her head, making me think of the wind chimes at Aunt Tuula's.

The fairies tending the fire, like the queen, were human-sized and had large wings. One wore a blue-green gown that changed hues like water in sunlight, and the other wore a dress that looked as if it were made of yellow and orange rose petals. The rosy fairy scattered petals around the two gigantic toadstools set back from the fire. When Queen Patchouli sat on the larger toadstool, its dome sank to form-fit around her. The mist flowed up to rest on her shoulders like a shawl.

I do not have a shy bone in my body, nor do I flinch when facing the unknown . . . usually. Aventurine, however, does not follow normal rules, and I wasn't certain how familiar or how formal I should be with the fairy queen. Birdie had been the center of her attention during my last visit. I stopped two feet back from the fire and waited while the fragrant smoke washed over me.

"Sit down, Kerka." Queen Patchouli patted the top of the smaller, spotted toadstool. "It's quite comfy, which seems especially appropriate, since the circumstances are not."

"They aren't?" I asked, taken aback. "Am I not supposed to be here?"

"Quite the contrary," Queen Patchouli said. "Your presence is essential, but we'll get to that later. There are other matters to attend to first. Sit down."

As I settled on the mushroom, it firmed up around me, and two fairies rushed over. One pulled my backpack from my hand and flew off. A glance from Queen Patchouli silenced my protests.

I knew my bag with my Kalis stick would be returned, but not having it bothered me. The other fairy brought me peach nectar in a daffodil cup and a cake made of sunflower seeds, nuts, and berries held together with honey. It was a small snack compared to the feast the fairies had served on Birdie's visit. Perhaps Queen Patchouli knew I had eaten a hot cross bun with cider before I fell asleep.

Queen Patchouli waited patiently, but when I swallowed the last bit of cake, she stood up. Gossamer swooshed, and the mist unraveled from her shoulders and drifted to the ground. A flurry of bees buzzed about in momentary disarray.

"We don't have another minute to lose," the queen said. "You must hurry, Kerka. Taking your time is not an option."

"What do you mean? How much time do I have?" I asked.

"I don't know. Follow me." Queen Patchouli's response left me no choice but to walk in her wake and trust that my questions would be answered when the queen was ready.

We swept to the center of the clearing on a path of fairy-flung rose petals. A grassy mound rose as we approached. Birdie and I had sat on willow chairs and eaten dinner at a table set atop a larger version of this rise. Only one woven willow chair stood by the table on the mound now, and the large leather-bound book — *The Book of Dreams* — was already in place.

Fairies came out of the willows as we walked, so that when I reached the chair, they hovered to my left and right, conveying the same sense of urgency I felt in Queen Patchouli's brisk pace. Without waiting to be told, I sat down and stared at the ancient book. The silver lettering on the cover seemed cast in the blue light of moonbeams even though the sun was now spilling over the tops of the trees into the clearing. Morning had come quickly.

"It's time to write your dreams, Kerka," Queen Patchouli said solemnly. She flicked her wrist, and the massive book opened to a blank page.

A fairy wearing a golden gown and a goldenrod wreath on her blond hair brought a peacock feather and a shell to the table. The feather was a quill pen. The shell had a blue lid made of fish scales. Inside was a pool of silvery blue ink.

"Reading the dreams of your ancestors is a privilege we usually bestow on our fairy-godmothers-in-the-making, but time is an important factor for you, Kerka." Sighing, Queen Patchouli looked uncharacteristically apologetic. "We dare not dally, and thus we will forego the ritual of writing your dream within a dream." Queen Patchouli bowed her head slightly. "You may begin."

I knew what the queen meant about dreams within dreams. I was a little disappointed not to get to read my family's dreams, but if there wasn't time, complaining wouldn't help. Hoping that if I wrote fast, there would be enough time to at least see my mother's entry, I picked up the quill pen. Dipping the pen in the ink, I wrote my dream, which was simply:

*I wish to bring my sisters
and myself back together.*

My handwriting was bold in the center of the page. I signed my name at the bottom and dated the page at the top.

I set down the pen. Birdie had told me that drawings, glitter stars, and lace had magically appeared on her page when she finished. My page remained as I had written it—a single, unadorned sentence. A twinge of disappointment faded when I realized that the presentation of my dream described me perfectly: to the point, with no frills.

"Finished already?" Sounding surprised, Queen Patchouli stepped closer. The fairies sitting on toadstools murmured softly and exchanged glances.

I held up my hand when a small picture of a squirrel appeared on a corner of the page. Suddenly drawings of fall leaves and acorns scrolled across the top of the page to a gray wolf in the other corner. The autumn foliage design changed into evergreen sprigs and pinecones down the outer edge of the page to a reindeer in the bottom corner. Green holly with red berries linked the reindeer to an elf wearing a red cap in the opposite corner, and interlaced blue icicles completed the border along the inside edge. Perhaps I wasn't so plain after all. When nothing else appeared, I lowered my hand. "*Now* it's finished."

"Very well, then," Queen Patchouli said, gathering the mist back around her. "Every girl who enters Aventurine has the chance to change things for the better here and in the real world. Although you are starting from behind, you've already proven your ability to face challenges and overcome them. Therefore, the time you did not spend writing your dream can be spent in the dreams of your ancestors."

I struggled not to grin, and Queen Patchouli pretended not to notice my struggle.

"Knowing the hearts and secrets of those who came before you in the Pax Lineage may help," said the queen. With a wave of her hand, the misty net floated free of her dress and turned blue as it settled over the table and me.

The tattered pages of *The Book of Dreams* began to turn, going faster and faster until they stopped suddenly on my mother's dream.

June 21, 1987

Tuula and I have been fighting for months. We are standing on opposite cliffs across a wide canyon screaming our different reasons why we are mad. My sister should be the one person in the world who understands me. Someone has to end this fight. I will wrap my "sorry" in a wind rope and throw it across the wide gulf to her. I will keep trying until Tuula and I cross our Kalis sticks again in honor of the Pax.

Britta

I never knew that my mother and aunt fought. I always thought of them as the two teenage girls in the photo with their arms around each other in their folk dancing outfits. My aunt had gone on to be a peacemaker for the U.N., but my mom was the quiet one, making her own kind of peace in our village in Finland, a helper of women, a part-time dance teacher, never expecting praise or notice.

Queen Patchouli closed the book with another wave of her hand. Then she led me to a spot under the magnificent magnolia tree. "You must change into proper fairy-made attire before you begin your mission."

"What *is* my mission?" I asked. I was anxious to know, but Queen Patchouli clearly wasn't ready to tell me.

"Clothes first." Pale blue fairy wings fluttered as the queen squared her shoulders and lifted her regal chin. Raising her arms like an orchestra conductor, she flicked her wrists again, pointing first to the right, then to the left.

Responding to the queen's command, vines sprouted from the ground in a circular pattern. Stems thickened and leaves widened as the vines grew and wove themselves into a large, overturned green basket with a doorway in the front. I watched as flowers blossomed over the canopy and streamers of morning glories grew downward, forming a curtain over the open doorway. A carpet of clover and violets blanketed the interior and stretched out to where I was standing. If Birdie had been there she would have laughed. The fairy queen liked things to be dramatic, and sometimes it was funny to what lengths she would go in order to create just the right effect.

"You'll find everything you need inside," Queen Patchouli told me. "Just open your backpack."

Thanking the fairy queen, I rushed down the flower path.

"Dress warmly!" Queen Patchouli called.

Eager to find my stick and get on with my quest, I pushed aside the morning glories and entered the garden dressing room. My backpack was nestled in the violet carpet at the back. Falling on my knees, I unbuckled it and immediately sprang clear when a thumping sound came from inside it. I scrambled backward and narrowly avoided being impaled by the wooden spire that zoomed upward out of my backpack. When the spire was ten feet tall, it began to unfold in a dozen different directions. Wood cracked and shuddered as panels slammed against each other until a completed wardrobe towered above me.

Getting to my feet, I faced the magical closet. A mountain-and-stag design that matched my backpack was carved into the double doors, along with a leopard's head framed by crossed Kalis sticks above the doors. The handles on the three drawers at the bottom of the wardrobe were shaped like cat's paws, proving once more that Aventurine was different for everyone, just as Zally had said. This wardrobe matched me, as Birdie's had matched her.

Remembering that time was critical, I opened the wardrobe. There were mirrors on the inside of both its doors, but it wasn't stuffed with fairy-made clothes for every imaginable occasion like Birdie's had been. Instead, everything I found was practical for winter and similar to things I had worn back home in Finland: pants and boots, sweaters and tops, coats, hats, mittens, and gloves in bright colors. No matter what I chose to wear, I would be warm and reminded of home—albeit a little more colorfully than I was used to dressing! I guess the fairies had to have fun, too.

I didn't mind not having too many choices; I liked wearing a school uniform so I didn't have to spend time deciding what to wear every day. I didn't waste a minute now. Peeling off my soccer uniform from the dream I didn't have, I put on orange cargo pants and tied them with a sash, then pulled on a soft blue long-sleeved T-shirt. I riffled through a short stack of sweaters and found a turtleneck in a dark raspberry with snowflakes on the cuffs. I picked socks that matched the sweater.

After I laced up a sturdy pair of hiking boots, I spent a little longer looking at the coats. I needed something warm but not too bulky. I chose a long turquoise coat made of a soft material I had never felt before. It was trimmed and lined with spotted faux fur, and an embroidered brambly design decorated the cuffs and hem. The instant I stuffed a pair of red mittens into the roomy coat pockets, the wardrobe collapsed twice as fast as it had formed. When the transformation was finished, the tip of my Kalis stick stuck out the top of my backpack.

A fairy dressed in violet came into the dome carrying a woven basket. She carefully folded her wings to fit through the doorway and held out the basket, saying, "These are for your journey." The basket contained a drawstring pouch, which looked like it was filled with food, and six large pea pods.

I took the pouch from the basket and put it in my backpack. Then I reached for the pea pods. I put five of them into my pack, then, curious, held the last one and started to poke at it gently.

"Don't!" the fairy warned, staying my hand. She took another small pod from her basket, held it up, and jabbed it with her finger. The pea pod expanded until it was as big as a zucchini. The stem end split open, and the fairy poured water from the pod into her hand. "Like magic," she said.

Or a big mess, I thought. But still, if handled correctly, it was amazingly useful and practical.

"Ready?" the fairy asked. I nodded and, draping the coat over my arm, followed her outside. When we cleared the doorway, the flowers on the canopy burst, creating a shower of colorful petal confetti. The vines untangled and retracted until they disappeared back into the ground.

Queen Patchouli sat in a swing made of weeping willow branches. When she rose to meet me, the branches untwisted and returned to their natural state. "You and your sisters are very different, and you are all missing a vital part of yourselves," the queen said. "Biba doesn't speak, and Rona is running away from her pain."

"What am *I* missing?" I couldn't think of anything.

"If your mission is successful, you'll find out," Queen Patchouli said.

"What is my mission?" I asked again.

"You must first find Biba's voice, Kerka. If you do, you should be able to discover and remedy the missing parts of yourself and Rona without too much difficulty. But if you fail to find Biba's voice, neither you nor Rona will be able to return to Aventurine. It is possible that Biba would have another chance for herself, but she is too young to know for sure now."

The quest seemed so unfair and outrageous, I couldn't help but say something. "How am I supposed to do *that*?" I asked. "Birdie had to find a stone and heal a blighted tree, things you can see and touch. And she had me to help her!"

Queen Patchouli watched me, her expression showing neither anger nor sympathy. "True," she said. "But each girl is different. You could not possibly expect to do something like Birdie's mission, something you have already come through. It only means something if it is a true challenge."

"But a voice has no substance!" I argued. "It is an impossible task. I am happy to climb mountains and swim rivers and run miles and—"

"You may do all those things as well, but they would be less challenging than what you have been asked to do," Queen Patchouli said, arching an eyebrow. "Now ask yourself, why would I send you on a mission you had no hope of completing?"

I saw the truth buried in her question. "You wouldn't," I answered sheepishly.

"The fairies of Aventurine exist to help fairy-godmothers-in-the-making achieve wisdom and control of their powers," Queen Patchouli reminded me. "I have something that will help you." She took a small blue pouch from the folds of her dress and pulled out a rope with three large knots in it. "These knots will help you control the wind, a Pax Lineage skill you haven't mastered yet but one you will need." Queen Patchouli handed the pouch to the violet fairy, who tied it to the leather thongs on my belt.

"Will I be able to ride the Redbird Wind again?" I asked hopefully. Birdie and I had ridden the mighty Redbird Wind together. It had felt just like flying, and I had loved every single second.

"No," Queen Patchouli said. "You'll be going elsewhere, and these knots work differently from the feathers."

"How about Zally's map?" I asked.

"You won't need the map," Queen Patchouli

said, softening her tone. "All you need are landmarks: Glass Lake, Three Queens, and a snowy mountain. You'll *know* the way."

I wasn't sure about that, but I hoped it was true. The directions sounded simple, but I knew it would be harder than it seemed. Still, there would be some mountain climbing, so that would be fun. I've always loved hiking, and snowy mountains didn't worry me. Plus I had the magic rope with knots, so I'd ride the wind somehow; now I was looking forward to just *starting*.

"Follow your instinct, and look for the Kalistonia Fairies." With those words, Queen Patchouli kissed my forehead. Then she turned in a swirl of green and walked into the woods, disappearing instantly. The remaining fairies followed her, vanishing, as well, into the foliage.

4

Three Paths Twice

I stood on the edge of the woods. Instinct. What did my instinct tell me? It told me to look around carefully and make an informed decision. I pulled aside the branches that the fairies had just gone through. There were three distinct trails going through the willows.

The left-hand path looked like it was covered with pine needles; the middle path was made of sand. A squirrel sat on the right-hand path, which was made of small gray pebbles, staring at me. I couldn't tell if it was the same squirrel I had met earlier, but it seemed like a sign. When the squirrel scampered down the path and then paused to look back, I made a decision. I followed the squirrel.

The little animal ran ahead of me, staying out of reach. It paused now and then, twisting its brown head around to make sure I was still there. The path wove on beyond the willow trees and through an evergreen forest strewn with rocks and ferns. As I walked, the air grew cooler, and I was just thinking about putting the coat on when I almost stumbled as the path became wide stone steps leading down to a large lake. The moment I stepped onto the lake's bank, the squirrel turned and darted back the way we had come.

"Good-bye!" I called, feeling suddenly alone. It was possible I would be by myself for this whole quest. It would have been nice to have someone with me, but I knew that I would be all right. This way, I could do exactly what I thought I needed to do without having to explain things to anyone. It could save a lot of time, being alone.

As I stared out over the lake, I realized what Queen Patchouli had said was true: I didn't need a map. The lake's surface was so still—like glass—and the pointed peaks of the three mountains on the far side of it were bathed in an unworldly golden glow. The mountains had to be the Three Queens, and the fairy-built raft of willow logs floating in the reeds would take me to where their slopes began.

I folded my coat and placed it on the raft beside a long pole. I wore my backpack so there was no chance of dropping it in the lake—unless I fell in. Aventurine is full of surprises, and something that looked safe could easily be dangerous. Large creatures might live in the lake or the calm water could suddenly become a tidal wave or a whirlpool. I had learned how to swim with Birdie, but I wasn't sure I'd be able to do it again without the river maidens' magic. I was thankful that at least the idea of swimming didn't bother me anymore, or this would have been a lot harder.

Gripping the sides of the raft with both hands, I pushed off. Jumping aboard just as it left shore, the tips of my toes touched the water. I didn't get far. Cattails and reeds along the banks snagged on both ends of the raft. Lying flat on the raft, I paddled with my hands until it floated free. Then I sat up and paused to get my bearings.

The fairies hadn't given me a paddle, but I could push the raft with the pole, at least until the lake got too deep. Shifting carefully, I looked over the raft's edge. The water was so clear, I could see everything in detail right down to the bottom of the lake. A translucent yellow fish with a rainbow top fin swam through plants with clear round leaves. A school of pink wiggly worms followed the fish.

Grabbing the pole, I stood so that my weight

was evenly distributed. The raft rocked a little on the quiet water, but I felt steady. I slipped the end of the eight-foot pole into the water and pulled it out when it touched bottom. Most of the pole remained dry, telling me that the water was shallow. I was still close to shore, though, so the water could get deeper in the middle.

Setting my sights on the three distant mountains, I put the pole back in the water and pushed. The raft moved forward. I pulled the pole partway up, jammed it into the bottom again, and pushed. After a few minutes, I settled into the rhythm of the poling motion—plunge, push, lift. It reminded me of music or playing a game. Every song, dance, or sport has a rhythm all its own. I can tell that I've got the hang of something new when the rhythm feels right.

But there's a downside, too. When I get into the zone of whatever I'm doing, it's like being lulled to sleep. So I wasn't ready when something yanked on the pole and almost pulled me into the water. I sat down hard and hung on to the pole—without it, I'd have to paddle with my hands all the way across the lake, and I didn't have time for that!

One of the logs the raft was made of was bigger around than the others. I pressed my heels against it for leverage and pulled the pole back. The thing in the water pulled harder and dragged me close to the raft's edge. I looked down at the water and saw beneath the surface a giant, flat bluish-green creature that looked like a stingray with pincers for a mouth. The pincers were clamped around my pole.

I played tug-of-war with the ray until my arms got tired. Pulling wasn't working, so I yanked the pole back and forth as fast as I could. The stingray didn't let go—instead, its pincers broke off as if they were made of glass! I felt terrible. I hadn't meant to hurt the creature.

I pulled the pole onto the raft. The ray hovered nearby, as though it were hoping the pole would come back. Just before it got bored and swam away, I saw the nubs of new pincers where the old ones had been. I touched the broken pincers on my pole. They felt like glass. I pried them off and held them up to the light. They really looked like glass. Queen Patchouli had used the name Glass Lake. Maybe the lake didn't just look like glass—maybe all the plants and creatures in the lake *were* glass!

When I started poling again, I kept looking down at the water as well as up at the mountains. Scanning the lake became part of the poling motion. I was alert for living creatures but not for other dangers. When I was halfway across, I pushed, expecting my pole to touch bottom. It didn't, and I almost fell off the raft. I didn't fall—I just sat down hard—but now I had another problem.

I didn't have a paddle, and the water was too deep for me to use the pole. The raft just bobbed. I was stuck lying down and paddling with my hands. Unfortunately, it turned out that my fingers looked like something tasty to eat and that the little glass fishies were scared of nothing. Although I paddled as fast as I could, I was nipped several times. I was so busy trying not to be fish food, a few minutes passed before I felt the breeze on my neck.

Looking up, I saw dark clouds scooting across the sky from behind me. In a moment the calm surface of the lake would be hit by the strong wind. Ripples were starting already, and if I didn't move fast, the raft could be swamped by waves! If I fell in the water, I doubted that my clothes would turn into a sleek wetsuit without the river maidens' magic—the weight of my boots alone would pull me down before I could possibly swim to shore!

I was just about to take my boots off, when I got an idea. It was crazy, but worth trying. I unfolded my coat and put it on, but I didn't fasten the buttons. I stood up, gripped the front edges, and held the coat open like a sail, facing the wind. The breeze seemed to embrace me as it filled the coat, and the coat's soft, strange material expanded as the wind filled it, turning it into a small sail. The wind in my sail-coat pushed the raft toward the far shore. I closed my eyes, the wind blowing in my face, as I raced the oncoming storm.

Bending my knees, I was able to ride the raft like a surfboard. I had no sooner settled into that rhythm than I was pelted by something. I opened my eyes to see flying fish, seemingly made of glass, zipping past me. The small fish weren't hitting me on purpose. We were going in the same direction, fleeing the storm. Most of the fish cleared both the raft and me, but the ones that hit me and fell to the hard logs shattered. Some left tiny cuts on my hands and neck before their school changed course and moved out of harm's way.

I sailed the raft the rest of the way across the lake—almost. The storm died out as quickly as it had risen, my coat shrank to its normal size, and I folded it back up. Then I used the pole to push the raft the last fifty yards to the beach. I jumped to the shore and hauled the raft onto the sand, stowing the pole underneath. Picking up my coat, I paused to look around.

The sandy beach was edged with large scattered rocks. Beyond the rocks was a wall of stones. The wall was quite high, and looked to be covered with moss of some sort. I wondered if I could climb it.

The three mountains were still some distance away, and I had to crane my neck to see the peaks. The golden glow over the tops of the Three Queens shone brilliantly even in daylight. With no other clues to consider, instinct and logic told me to head toward the mountains.

A clickety-click sound grabbed my attention just as something pinched my left boot. Startled, I looked down. A six-inch crablike creature had clamped on to my foot with a large claw. The crab's eyes, which were attached to floppy three-inch stalks, stared back at me like those of a small alien. The other claw made a clicking noise as the creature repeatedly opened and snapped it closed. My boot's leather was thick enough to protect my toes from the crab's pincers, but shaking my foot didn't dislodge the little beast. I would have thought a creature made of glass might be a little more careful about who it grabbed!

"You've bitten off way more than you can chew, little guy." I shook my finger at the creature as I scolded it. Then I blinked and smiled, inspired by my own words. "But I have something that's much tastier than my boot."

Being careful not to poke the water pods, I opened the food pack and broke off a small piece of what looked like a cake made of sunflower seeds and carefully placed it on top of my boot. The crab's eyes atop their floppy stalks stopped jiggling as they studied my offering, but the crab didn't let go or try to grab the cake. Anxious to get moving, I tried stamping my heel to jar the creature loose, but the claw clamped down tighter, and it hung on.

The crab's one-claw clickety-click taunt became a noisy clatter as more crabs suddenly swarmed to joined the chorus. Interestingly enough, not a single one skittered near the rocks.

I was wondering if I would have to just break its little claw off—hoping that it would grow a new one like the stingray—when I tried one last idea. Walking on the heel of my left boot so I wouldn't break the crab, I slowly made my way to a large rock. As soon as I climbed onto it, the crab let go of my boot, dropped into the sand, and scurried back to the crab-creature colony.

From here I was right beside the stone wall. The moss was more of a slime—so although there appeared to be places where I could put a hand or foot, the wall was too slippery to climb. Switching the heavy coat to my other arm, I jumped to the next big rock. I headed down the beach this way, looking for a break in the stone wall. I had to get over it to reach the Three Queens.

Suddenly I remembered the knotted wind rope. I couldn't climb the barrier, but a strong wind could carry me over. I opened the blue drawstring pouch and pulled out the rope. Just as I was about to touch the first knot, I asked myself: Was it wise to use one of the magic knots so soon?

I put the rope back in its pouch. Then I took a piece of cake from the other pouch and nibbled as I continued jumping from rock to rock. I found cracks between boulders here and there, but they were too narrow for anything except a butterfly flying sideways to squeeze through. Looking up, I realized that the rock wall blocked my view of the Three Queens. On the off chance that seeing the crowned peaks would give me a brainstorm, I jumped off the rock.

I braced to jump back on in case any crabs attacked me from the sand. Keeping an eye out, I hurried down the beach, walking away from the rocks until the golden peaks of the three mountains were visible. From here, I could also make out three distinct paths leading up to the piles of rocks: One went straight and the others branched to the left and right. Each path was obviously a route to one of the Three Queens, and each path was blocked by a pair of humungous boulders.

One of the mountains was the key to completing my quest and making my dream come true, but which one? I had no information, no map to help me decide, and not even a friend to talk to about it.

A shrill whistle rang out as pebbles and small rocks tumbled down the boulder barrier.

"Who's there?" I yelled.

Suddenly a small man jumped out of the rocks. Standing two feet tall and wearing what I thought of as basic elf clothing—red cap, brown leggings, a green coat with white fur trim, and black boots—he watched me from atop a large rock. His pointed ears were too long to fit under his cap.

I was sure he was an elf. He looked seriously grumpy, and I tried not to be too worried. In Finnish folklore, disturbing an elf is almost as bad as insulting or cheating one.

The elf's ears twitched when he cocked his head. I just stared back until he somersaulted off his perch. The little man rocked up onto his feet and zipped across the sand, moving so fast I saw only a blur of red and green, like a piece of Christmas gone crazy. He skidded to a halt in front of me.

"Who are you?" I asked.

"Who's who? And who are you?" the elf answered in a squeaky lilt. Then he added with a smirk, "As if I didn't know!"

I wasn't sure whether to tell him my name — which would give the elf the upper hand — or to call his bluff, which might not *be* a bluff.

"Who am I, then?" I asked with an impish grin, and crossed my arms, daring him. I knew that elves have a habit of getting even by doing something ten times worse than what was done to them. But they also like to be amused and entertained — that's what I was shooting for.

The elf jumped up and down and spoke in jumbled rhyme. "The name I choose is Kerka Laine. So I win, you lose; I know your name."

My mouth dropped open, but I quickly closed it. The fairies must have told him to expect me.

"Don't hesitate or you'll be late!" The elf leaned toward me, his brow furrowing. "Your task must be finished, over and done, before the Three Queens' glow disappears in the sun." He waved his hand in the direction of the horizon.

"By morning?" I asked, perplexed.

"Maybe." The elf shrugged.

I asked a different question, hoping to get a clearer answer. "How long do I have?"

"Tomorrow, today. It's hard to say."

"What does that mean?" I asked as evenly as I could. I couldn't let myself get riled up.

The elf threw up his hands. "Sometimes the sun rises, sometimes it blinks on. Or takes the day off, and there isn't a dawn." Then he concluded in an ominous tone: "In Aventurine, anything goes, and no one, but no one, ever knows."

I exhaled slowly. So no one in Aventurine knew when the golden glow on the Three Queens would be lost in sunlight, because the sun didn't always follow the rules. But it didn't matter. I still had to find my little sister's voice before dawn, whenever it happened. I had to have time to finish. Otherwise, my mission would be a fool's errand, and Queen Patchouli was no fool. But now I had to go as fast as possible in case there was exactly enough time and not a minute more, which brought me back to my original problem.

"Thank you," I said to the elf. "That is very

helpful information. So can you tell me which path I should take?" I asked as respectfully as I could, trying to get elf points. "You seem to know so many things."

"What trade can you make?" the elf asked.

In stories, elves never do something for nothing, and they are willing to barter for both honor and treats. It was a good thing the Willowood Fairies had given me food for the journey. "I have a honey bar." I took a bar from my pouch and held it out.

"Secondhand fairy food? That's rude!" he spoke with a look of disdain.

"It's perfectly good and very sweet!" I said, a little taken aback.

The elf leaned toward me again. "You can give a fairy's gift away, but not for a bargain on any day."

"Really?" I asked, truly surprised. "I had no idea. Well, I don't have anything to trade, then. The fairies gave me everything I have, except my backpack."

The elf sniffed. "One more thing is yours to give, your Kalis stick will always live."

I was starting to feel a little grouchy myself. "I'll get lost in Aventurine or risk being expelled forever before I'll part with my Kalis stick," I said. This actually seemed to be the right tone for the elf.

"So wise are you, and honorable, too." The elf

paused, rubbing his pointy chin as he considered our dilemma. "No trade means I cannot tell you which path to take, but I'll give a hint for a favor's sake."

"So if I do you a favor, we're even?" I asked.

The elf nodded. "Take a message to my brother, then nothing more will we owe one another."

"And how will I find him?" I could not agree to anything that would take time or divert me from my quest.

"He'll find you, if your path be true," the elf answered.

"Then I agree," I said.

The elf motioned for me to come closer, and when I leaned down he said quietly, as if someone might be listening, "Tell him that if the wind goes free, so will we."

"That's easy enough to remember," I said.

Then the elf kept his word and gave me the hint. He pointed to the mountain on the left and said, "Hourling for grace." Then he pointed to the middle mountain and said, "Dayling for the brave." He pointed to the last mountain. "Yearling for the serene." He dropped his arm. "Only one will save your place in Aventurine."

I laughed; this was a good hint for me. I was certain I knew what it meant. The Kalis sticks my mother gave my sisters and me each had a letter carved into them, but the letters didn't match our names. Aiti had said only: *"You will know why when the time is right."* The time was right now—my stick was carved with a *D.* "I'll take the path to Dayling," I said.

"And the message, too. Don't forget, will you?" asked the elf.

"I won't forget," I assured him.

The little man leaped into the air and clapped his hands. He was gone in a flash, laughing as he bounded toward the boulders.

5

Stalking the Tree Line

The ground shook and I heard a thunderous rumbling and grating sound. The stone wall was separating, making a space I could slip through. I didn't know how long it would stay that way, so I slung the coat over my shoulder and ran, blood pounding in my ears, and my boots pounding on the sand.

When I was six feet from the opening, the wall stopped moving. The opening was barely wide enough for me to squeeze through sideways. With rock pressing me front and back, I sucked my breath in as I forced my way through. My coat dragged on the ground, and the hem caught on something I couldn't see. I tugged, then pulled, to free it while I kept squeezing through the narrow opening. I pushed so hard to clear the stones that I landed in a bramble of berries when I fell through the gap.

The two halves of the wall slammed together behind me. I stared at the towering wall with a strange sense of calm. I was out of breath and I was scraped and scratched, but I had survived. My mother had carved a *D* on my Kalis stick. She must have known I would be making this journey.

Biba's voice and my destiny lay ahead—on the mountain called Dayling.

I gathered up my heavy coat with a sigh. It was a pain to carry, but I couldn't leave it behind. I knew I would need it before the end of the journey. Still, I *had* to find a safer, more convenient way to carry it.

Wearing the coat thrown over my shoulders wouldn't work. The path ahead was clogged with brambles and branches and the cloth would snag. But maybe I could carry the coat in my backpack if I could somehow make it small enough. That didn't seem possible, but I tried anyway. To my surprise, the coat got smaller and smaller every time I folded it. Chiding myself for not taking magic into account, I kept folding until the coat was the size of my father's wallet. Then, with the coat neatly stowed with my food pouch and Kalis stick, I set off on the rocky path to Dayling Mountain.

The trail twisted and turned around more boulders and tall trees dripping with hanging moss. I was glad I had on winter clothes when I crawled through a tunnel of briar and prickly vines that scratched my hands and face. Hundreds of spiders were building webs in the twisted branches. I didn't mind spiders, but the possibility that one could fall into my hair gave me chills. I jumped when a six-legged red lizard with three glowing green eyes tickled my ear with its blue triple-forked tongue.

I didn't notice the gradual incline until I cleared the tangles of vegetation and emerged on a barren slope strewn with rocks and scrub brush. I trudged upward toward a tree line. With no one to talk to on this easy path, I started wondering if all fairy god-mothers are connected by fairy magic and could be called upon when needed. Maybe that's why I had been drawn into Birdie's dream quest: she needed my charge-ahead attitude and get-it-done-no-matter-what methods. Or maybe it was something else, something less obvious. Birdie had told me that de-spite our differences, having me along made the mis-sion seem less scary. I wished that someone would show up to help me, but wishing wouldn't make it so.

Nothing moved on the rocky incline, and the

silence was unsettling. To take my mind off it, I thought back to the day my mother gave me the Kalis stick, a year ago. . . .

The garden and lawn behind our house were bathed in summer light. Being the middle child, I stood between my sisters as my mother handed each of us a short colored stick.

"What is it, Aiti?" Seven-year-old Biba held the blue stick like a magic wand, her eyes wide with wonder.

"It's a Kalis stick," Aiti said, "the talisman of our family and the Pax Lineage."

I ran my fingers over the smooth wood of my orange stick and traced the graceful *D* carved into one end. Rona's green stick was marked with a *Y*.

"How come mine has an *H* on it?" Biba asked, echoing my thoughts. "My name doesn't start with *H*."

"No, it doesn't, darling," Aiti said, smiling. "You'll understand someday."

"What does it do?" Rona studied her stick, turning it over and over in her hands and frowning as though she had been given a puzzle too complex or too silly to solve.

"Whatever you tell it," Aiti explained, "but first you must learn the language of Kalis from Kalistonia."

Biba gasped with delight. "The sticks speak?"

"They sing when you dance." Aiti picked up a rose-colored stick two feet longer than ours. She leaped into the air.

We watched in awe as our mother glided, spun, twirled, and leapt through, over, and around the garden. One second she was ducking as though to avoid an invisible threat and the next she was bounding across the lawn, leaping higher than I believed possible. Her Kalis stick sang as she sliced it through the air or twirled it about her head and shoulders like a sword. When she finished, we begged to learn the beautiful, energetic dance.

"Learning Kalis is a slow process that requires dedication and discipline," Aiti told us solemnly, "and the advanced parts can only be learned in Aventurine. You must practice the basic steps until they become as natural as breathing before you can go. We'll begin with Peek from Behind the High Grass."

My mother held the ends of the Kalis stick in her hands at arm's length. She raised the stick to eye level, then shifted her arms and the stick to the right, then to the left. She repeated the move several times, performing it precisely the same way every time. The next variation was more complicated. In a fluid motion, she drew her left leg back, released the left end of the stick, and leaned forward as she flicked the stick outward with her right hand. Then she performed the step flicking the stick to the left.

"When you can Peek from Behind the High Grass without wobbling or hesitating, I'll teach you Stroking the Water Horse's Mane." With that, she tucked her Kalis stick under her arm and left us to practice.

I could still smell the gardenias my mother wore twined in her braids, and the memory made me smile. By nightfall that same day, I had learned to snap the stick outward, to lean and shift to the other side without losing my balance.

Now the sun rose higher in the sky; it felt good to be striding along, but I ticked off the minutes in my head. When I reached the tree line, I gave one last backward glance before I entered the dark woods. From that viewpoint, the Glass Lake was a brilliant blue near the Three Queens beach, but further out, the water darkened and blended into a mist that obscured the Willowood bank.

Suddenly a noise snapped me back to full alert. In the quiet, the sound of a breaking twig had the same effect as the boom and crack of thunder and lightning: I froze. Had an animal stepped on the twig or was it something else? Was the animal small or big, vicious or harmless? Was the "something else" sinister or good? Was it a person or a thing, ordinary or magical?

I focused on a rustle of dry brush behind a large pine tree straight ahead. Then I glimpsed a flash of movement to my right and swiveled to look. There was nothing to see except tree trunks, fallen branches, and dark spaces where sunlight couldn't penetrate the thick canopy of leaves above. A stirring to one side caught me off guard, and I spun toward the sound of footsteps muted by damp leaves and moss. A shadow darted between the trees.

I felt goose bumps pop out as I took cover behind a large tree with rough sunset red bark. Bracing to fight, I reached back to pull my Kalis stick out of my backpack. Several seconds passed before I found the wooden end. Ten predators could have attacked before my fingers finally curled around the stick. Breathless and shaken, I turned to scan the woods, but no beasts charged out of the dark with fangs and claws bared.

I had not been in danger after all. Even with no witnesses, I was embarrassed. "So stop acting like a helpless twit and get it together before a real monster turns you into Kerka snacks," I said aloud. The sound of my voice echoed in the silent forest, but it bolstered my courage. I put my Kalis stick back into my backpack. After making sure I could grab it quickly next time, I plunged deeper into the woods.

As I walked, it became so dark I could barely see the path. I looked up and saw that the foliage above was packed too tightly to let much light shine through. I had to go so slowly and carefully that it was painful. But I had no choice—I couldn't go back.

After a long trek, the gray of Aventurine's twilight broke through the dense bower again. I headed toward the light. The instant I could see my feet on the path, I stopped—and just in time. I was one step away from a cliff that dropped straight down for hundreds of feet! I studied the sheer cliff wall on the far side of the chasm. Vertical black-and-red ridges sparkled, as though someone had painted them with glitter. I turned and followed the path along the ridge with the golden glow, the mountain summit in sight.

As the forest trees began to thin out, the path veered away from the cliff, becoming visible again. No longer in danger of falling, I considered taking a break to have a drink and eat a sunflower cake. Those comforts were put on hold when a chomping noise brought me to another sudden halt.

I waited, listening. The cadence changed every

few seconds, like a cow chewing its cud. Eager to see another living creature, I decided to find out what it was and hurried down the path to a clearing. The grassy oasis was bordered on one side by the striped cliff. Heavy stands of trees formed the other sides of what looked like a star-shaped clearing. I crept to a break in the trees to scout the situation first.

A brown reindeer with magnificent antlers stood in the center of the clearing, chewing grass and yellow buttercups. Long golden hair flowed from the underside of her neck, and a stubby tail flicked at nonexistent flies. Of all the deer species in the world, only female reindeer grow antlers as big as males. I did a report on reindeer when I was in fifth grade, but I'd never seen one this close. The size of a large pony, the reindeer turned to stare at me. Rising, I stepped out of hiding and met her liquid brown gaze.

"Who are you?" I asked as though she could answer.

Just then a low, menacing growl came from the edge of the trees. The reindeer stiffened, and I saw the wolf. Silver gray with streaks of black around its ears, eyes, and muzzle, the wolf was poised to charge. It held my gaze with golden eyes as wary as the reindeer's eyes were innocent. Its fangs gleamed in the twilight, and a snarl warned of an attack.

Eyes white with terror, the reindeer snorted and pranced. Her instinct was to flee, but neither she nor I could outrun the wolf. I scanned our surroundings. The trail disappeared into the tall grass, but my eyes had no trouble following its route through the clearing. Plants bent to each side of the trail, like hair parted in the middle. The slight hope I felt was quickly dashed when I saw where the path led: straight off the cliff.

My mind calculated quickly. To stay on the Dayling path and escape the wolf, the reindeer and I had to reach the far side of the canyon. It was a hundred yards across, way too far to jump.

Growling again, the wolf took a step forward.

The reindeer trembled. "You have to save me."

The animal's sweet, frightened voice startled me.

"It looks so hungry." The reindeer whispered urgently, "Please, do something."

"Be quiet and let me think," I said softly.

My Kalis stick would be as useless as a toothpick against the wolf's massive jaws, and my cakes would only be an appetizer. In a flash I remembered the knotted rope and Queen Patchouli's assurance that as a member of the Pax Lineage, *I could control the wind.*

As the wolf took another step toward me, I opened the pouch, removed the rope, and moved closer to the reindeer. I had no idea what to do, but I touched the first knot.

A whistling sound rose from the depths of the forest.

"What's that?" the reindeer asked, pressing against me. She was warm and soft, and it felt good.

"I think it's our ride." I winced as the shrill sound grew louder. The wolf crouched down as tree trunks shuddered, and branches swayed when a ribbon of wind tore through the woods. It ripped into the clearing and scooped the reindeer and me off the ground as if we were dry leaves.

The wolf sprang forward, slashing at my boots and the reindeer's hooves with teeth and claws. The wind made a sudden shift upward, lifting us out of reach. The wolf fell back to the ground with an angry howl.

"I can't look!" Closing her eyes, the reindeer tucked her chin and drew up her dangling legs.

Airborne and safe from our pursuer, I whooped as the ribbon of wind whisked us over the edge of the cliff. I looked down, but we were so high, there wasn't much to see. The black-and-red ridges on the cliff walls faded into a sparkling brown haze. I didn't care. The speed of the wind was breathtaking, and for a few moments, my troubles were forgotten.

The reindeer and I were passengers in the wind's palm. When it curled to drop us gently on the ground, I looked back across the chasm. The wolf prowled the rim of the other side, padding back and forth. I held its gaze until it gave up and vanished into the woods.

"Is it gone?" the reindeer asked.

"I think so," I said uneasily. Somehow I was certain, the wolf was what had been following me since I first entered the forest. It would not give up easy prey that had barely escaped, but the reindeer seemed so innocent and fragile, I didn't want to worry her.

"You'll be far, far away before the wolf finds a way across the chasm." I put the rope back in the pouch then, and out of habit, I double-checked to make sure my Kalis stick was still in my backpack. It was.

"Did you say, 'I'll be far away'?" The reindeer's ears perked forward. "Where will *you* be?"

"Up there." I pointed toward the golden peak of

Dayling Mountain, which was closer but still a long way off.

"That *is* far away," the reindeer said. She glanced at me with a puzzled look. "Where are we?"

"In Aventurine; it's a dream world," I answered. "I'm Kerka. Who are you?"

"If I have a name, I don't know it. I don't even know how I came to be in this place. I must be lost." The reindeer bent her head and grabbed a tuft of grass.

"Me too, but in a different way," I said. "I know where I am, but nothing has felt right since my mother died."

"I don't remember my mother," the reindeer said, "but being with you feels right to me."

That wasn't a surprise. I had just saved the reindeer from being slaughtered by a wolf.

"It feels right to me, too," I said automatically as I looked around for the path.

"Oh, good!" The reindeer lifted her head. "If I go with you, we both won't be alone anymore."

"What?" My head jerked up. "You can't come with me."

The reindeer hung her head. "Why can't I? You said it feels right to you, right?"

"It's a very long journey," I explained as gently

as I could. I didn't want to hurt her feelings. "I can't ride the wind to get there. I have to walk."

"I have four legs," the reindeer argued. "You only have two."

"I'm on a dangerous mission," I countered.

"Please, please, take me with you," the reindeer pleaded.

I stared at her. I could probably get used to her timid, jittery manner. I guessed that I wouldn't mind having company, but I had wished I had someone to *help* me complete my quest, not someone who needed *my* help.

The reindeer's liquid eyes looked like they were filling with tears, then she turned away. No matter how tough I was, I couldn't say no. I simply couldn't do it.

I sighed. "Okay, you can come with me," I told the reindeer. "But you have to keep up."

"I will!" The reindeer shook her antlers, then lowered her head to graze.

Suddenly it hit me that I was talking to a reindeer! My head was filled with questions. Was she enchanted or did all reindeer in Aventurine talk? Then I remembered that plants talked to Birdie. Apparently, reindeer liked to talk to me. At least she didn't speak Latin.

I looked up at the sky. The sun didn't seem to have moved since the last time I looked, but eventually night would fall, and then dawn.

"Time to go," I told the reindeer.

"But I'm not finished eating," she said.

"You are if you're coming with me!" I turned and headed off down the path. I had learned long ago that the best way to win an argument is to not let it start.

"Then I'm not coming!" the reindeer shouted.

"Okay." I kept walking without glancing back. I had to be firm. Besides, I knew what I was doing. The poor reindeer didn't even know her name.

Behind me, the reindeer snorted. Another minute passed before her good judgment won out over her stomach. She trotted up behind me just as the path entered another forest.

"You're mean," the reindeer said, pouting.

"No, I'm on a mission," I said calmly. "I have things I have to do."

6

The Icefall

We walked along together companionably. The woods on this side of the chasm were nothing like the dark forest. Slender trees with twisting branches and large trees with rough bark grew farther apart from one another. Clusters of purple, lavender, and pink violets huddled between tree roots, and blue mushrooms with gold spots dotted the leaves and pine needles that covered the forest floor.

"Don't eat the blue mushrooms," the reindeer said when we walked by a large crop of them. "They smell funny."

"I won't." I looked back and smiled. I didn't smell anything, but reindeer have highly sensitive noses. "Thanks for the warning, R.D."

"Who's R.D.?" the reindeer asked.

"You are," I said. "I have to call you something,

so I'll call you R.D. It's short for reindeer. Get it?"

The reindeer snorted again. "Why can't I have a real name?"

I exhaled with exasperation. "Do you like this? A-r-d-e-e, Ardee."

"Oh, yes!" The reindeer laughed and bobbed her head. "I like that *much* better."

"Good." I patted Ardee's neck and tried not to giggle.

We continued on, walking side by side when the path was wider and single file when it narrowed. The path itself was lined with spindles of silver lichen. I stayed on the alert. Lizards and fist-sized furry-ball creatures scurried up and down tree trunks and across ivy-covered branches just above my head. Silver snakes curled around higher branches, watching us with languid curiosity as we passed underneath. And above the snakes, blackbirds flitted from limb to limb or sat on nests.

My breath caught in my throat when something crashed through the trees behind me. I drew my Kalis stick and spun as Ardee reared back and cried, "Help!"

Primed to repel an attack, I lowered my stick and watched the reindeer flail about, tossing her head and bleating in panic. She was trying to shake off a bushy branch that was caught in her antlers.

"Get it off!" Ardee yelped. "Get it off!"

"Stand still!" I ordered. "It's just a branch."

Ardee stop struggling and stood with her front legs splayed and her head down. "It's not just a branch. Something's living in it! Hurry!"

The branching tree limb was wedged so tightly I couldn't budge it. I raised my Kalis stick, hoping a sharp whack would jar the branch loose or break it. Just before I swung, I heard a tiny ripping sound. Taking a closer look, I noticed a large silvery gray cocoon nestled in the fork of the main branch. I couldn't hit or break the branch without crushing it.

"There's nothing to worry about, Ardee," I whispered, "but you have to stay still for a minute."

"Okay, but take the branch off," the reindeer pleaded.

"I can't," I whispered louder this time. I didn't want to scare the creature trying to free itself from the cocoon. I hoped it was harmless, but I didn't know. "Just trust me, please."

I put my free hand on Ardee's quivering back, then slid my arm over her. The reindeer stopped shaking and stood quietly, her chin resting on the ground and her hide rippling with twitches. It felt good to know that I could make her feel better so easily. I just hoped I'd be able to protect her if what came out of the cocoon was something unpleasant. I held my Kalis stick ready. I watched as the split in the cocoon widened.

A silver and black moth slowly slipped out of the casing, unfolding wings as delicate and transparent as those of a fairy. It was the biggest moth I'd ever seen. It was at least eight inches from the tip of its head to the end of its thorax. The silvery wings dried quickly. When the moth flew away, I broke the branch, took the pieces off Ardee's antlers, and put my Kalis stick back in my backpack.

Ardee watched the moth drift through the woods, all fear forgotten. "It's so pretty! Where is it going?"

"Toward the light," I said, pointing down the trail. The glow of twilight shone brighter ahead, unobstructed by trees. I broke into a run. Although she could have easily pushed past me at any time, I noticed that Ardee stayed behind me until we emerged from the woods into a huge meadow.

"Happy!" Kicking up her heels, the reindeer ran in circles through long, lush grasses and wildflowers. Her joy made me grin, it was so full and real.

"Come on, Kerka!" she called. "Run with me!"

I was about to say that I had to plan my next

move when I thought, *What can a few minutes hurt?*
Then I ran into the grasses and wildflowers. We
played tag, and I made Ardee and myself flower
wreaths, thinking I'd have to tell Birdie about them.
It was the happiest and freest that I had felt in such
a long time. Finally Ardee said, "I'm hungry!" before
she stopped and put her head down to graze, her
wreath slipping over one ear as she ate.

Rolling my eyes, I let the reindeer eat while I
figured out where to go next. Tall, cylindrical stones
marked the path ahead, each one placed within view
of the next. The route ran straight and true through
the meadow to a field of what looked like glimmering
snow. Dayling Mountain towered over the blanket
of blue-white with the flanking peaks of Hourling
and Yearling barely visible behind it. I could still see
the golden aura around the three peaks.

I carefully took a pea pod out of my backpack.
"Are you thirsty?" I asked the reindeer.

Ardee snapped her head up and blinked. "I
don't smell water anywhere, but I would very much
like a drink. Can you make magic water like you
make magic wind?"

"Sort of." I laughed, then I poked the pod until it expanded and the top split. I raised it to drink.

"Water!" The excited reindeer lunged and hit my chest with her antlers.

"Oof!" The air whooshed out of my lungs as I landed flat on the ground with my arms out. With empty lungs and a reindeer on top of me, I couldn't breathe or move or stop the water from pouring out of the pod.

"Oops." Ardee winced and jumped off me.

I couldn't talk until my breath came back. When I was breathing normally again, I got to my feet, brushed myself off, and dangled the empty green pod in front of the reindeer's nose. "This isn't an 'oops.' This is a very *big* problem."

"I'm sorry." Ardee's voice was small. "I've never seen a magic water bottle before, and I'm really thirsty."

"So am I." My voice was tight. "You wasted a whole pod of water! We only have *five* left, and now I have to open *another* one so we don't get dehydrated and pass out. Then we'll only have *four*, and I don't know how far we have to go to find more water—if we find water."

Ardee sniffled.

I took a deep breath. Being angry wouldn't

change anything. I took more deep breaths until I relaxed. Then I took another pod from my backpack and held my hand by the reindeer's face, palm out. "Do not move until I say so."

"Okay," Ardee said meekly.

I jabbed the pod, took a long drink, and then gave the rest to Ardee. I poured it into her mouth a little at a time so none was spilled. When the water was gone, I buried both pods. They would fertilize the meadow as they decomposed. Birdie would like that, too.

Of course, Ardee started grazing again, but I went down the path, checking the rope pouch as I walked. "We have to keep going, Ardee. Come on!"

"But I'm hungry," Ardee grumbled as she trotted along behind me.

"Then graze as you go," I said. "You can walk and eat at the same time, can't you?"

"I guess. But it doesn't taste as good that way." Sighing, the reindeer paused to nose through the grass, looking for a tasty mouthful. "Wait for me, Kerka!"

I spun around and pointed toward Dayling summit. "I have to be on top of that mountain by a certain time," I told her. "It's extremely important to me. You can keep up, or you can stay here. Which is it going to be?"

"Keep up," the reindeer said. She pulled up a mouthful of grass and jogged to close the space between us.

Despite the fact that Ardee paused every few minutes to grab another bite of pasture, we reached the far side of the meadow in good time. The sun was getting lower, and the mountain cast shadows on a wide expanse of white just ahead. What I had thought was a field of snow turned out to be a huge mound of ice that stretched toward the mountains as far as I could see. It looked just like the glaciers in Finland. This was actually good because the icy surface would be hard to walk on but not as dangerous as trying to slog through deep snow.

"We'll stop here a few minutes," I said, moving several yards back into the meadow. I didn't need to rest, but I knew that Ardee had to eat as much as possible before we went on. Reindeer live off their extra body fat during the harsh winter months; I just hadn't realized exactly how much they had to consume! I knew that where we were going grass would be as hard to find as unfrozen water.

"I like you, Kerka," Ardee said, lowering her head to eat.

"I like you, too, Ardee," I replied, smiling.

"This is the best"—tug, chew—"grass"—tug, chew—"I've ever tasted," Ardee mumbled through mouthfuls.

"It might be the *last* grass you taste for a while," I said. "There's nothing but snow and ice in front of us as far as I can see."

"I don't like ice," Ardee said.

"What?" I said in surprise. "But you're a reindeer. Ice and snow are your natural habitat."

"That doesn't mean I have to like it." Ardee snorted and resumed eating.

I was impatient but didn't rush her. I reminded myself that she was young. And I also started thinking that even if she held me back a bit, somehow she was helping me. That she was to me what I was to Birdie. And, honestly, she just made me feel good.

Reaching into my backpack, I pulled out my coat. The garment returned to full size as I unfolded it and spread it on the grass. I sat down and ate a

honey bar and one sunflower seed cake while I studied the golden snowcapped mountain. I was pretty
sure we had reached the halfway point. I wasn't full
when I finished eating, but I had to ration my sup-
plies. I decided to let Ardee continue grazing a few
more minutes. We had a long way to go, and she
would need her strength.

"What!" I sat up with a start, horrified when I realized I had dozed off. The reindeer was standing at
my side with her nose in my face. Her moist nostrils
flared slightly, and she stared at me intently. "How
long have I been asleep?"

"I don't know," the reindeer answered.

"Why didn't you wake me?" I asked, scrambling
to my feet. I was upset about losing precious time.

"You were asleep," the reindeer said. As I was
about to argue, she explained, "I only sleep when I'm
tired. You can't climb a winter mountain if you're
tired, so I was very careful not to wake you."

"Okay, thanks." I couldn't be mad at her for
thinking of me. I noticed she wasn't eating any longer.
"Are you full?" I asked her. I could hardly believe it.

Ardee bobbed her head, rattling her antlers.
"For now."

"Good," I said.

I took the mittens out of the coat pocket and put them on. Then I slipped into the coat and noticed that it had grown a hood. Wondering if it had the power to respond to the actual climate, I zipped it up. Then I took off my crushed flower wreath and pulled the hood up over my head. I put my backpack on over the coat and adjusted my Kalis stick so I could grab it in a hurry. As I started briskly across the last stretch of meadowland, Ardee uncharacteristically galloped ahead and waited at the glacier.

"Why are you in such a hurry?" I asked. "I thought you didn't like ice."

"I know a trick!" Ardee announced proudly. "It will help us."

"What is it?" I asked, intrigued.

The reindeer bent her front leg. "See the bottom of my hoof?"

I humored her and looked. The big pad in the center of the hard hoof wall was soft and cushy. "I see it."

"Watch this." Ardee sprang onto the glacier.

"What?" I asked impatiently. The ice was slippery and it took me a minute to reach her side.

"Hold on to my fur so you don't fall, then look at my hoof again."

Ardee bent her leg at the ankle and rested the toe of her hoof on the ice so I could see the underside. The big pad had shrunken and hardened within the hoof wall, leaving the hoof with a cookie-cutter rim. When I looked up, she stomped on the slick glacier. Her hoof cut into the ice, and she didn't slip or slide.

"Wow!" I was truly impressed. "Is that magic or natural?"

Ardee moved her head from side to side slightly, the reindeer version of a shrug. "Maybe magic makes winter feet happen faster here."

Tightening my grip on the reindeer's long hair, I held on as she moved forward. The ridged soles on my boots gave me some purchase on the ice, but not enough to keep me from sliding on the slippery spots.

"Can you see the path, Ardee?"

"Yes, I have winter eyes now, too." Ardee turned her head. Her brown summer eyes had changed to blue.

Being dependent on Ardee made me feel strange. Then it occurred to me that I didn't feel odd about depending on magical knots or an enchanted map, so how was depending on a living creature any different? I tried to keep this in mind as Ardee moved at a very slow pace, testing every step on the hazardous ice. I didn't object. I could not have crossed the glacier as easily or as fast without her, and my woolen coat did not keep out the cold completely. Pressing close to Ardee's side kept me warm as well as upright. My fingers were cold even though I was wearing mittens. Burying my hands in the reindeer's thick undercoat helped.

"Don't let go," said Ardee. "I really don't want to lose you."

"Don't worry," I replied. "I don't want to lose you, either. You're doing a great job," I added. "I couldn't do this without you."

"Really?" she asked.

"Yes, really," I said. "But we can't talk anymore, okay? It's much too cold and we have to make it all the way across."

We plodded across the white expanse in silence. I kept my head down to protect my face. Numbed by cold and lulled by the slow, steady rhythm of our progress, I lost all track of time. I was taken by surprise when we came to a halt at a wall of ice. From a distance, it had looked like part of the glacier.

"What is it?" Ardee asked, sounding both fearful and annoyed.

"A frozen waterfall," I said. I looked up but I

couldn't see the top of the gigantic icicle. "My dad calls them icefalls."

The reindeer followed my gaze. "There's no way I can climb it."

I had already reached the same conclusion.

"What are we going to do?" The reindeer's voice quivered.

"Don't worry," I said softly. "I'll think of something." Every problem had a solution, even in Aventurine. I had solved the elf's riddle and opened the boulder gate. And Queen Patchouli's magic rope had summoned the wind to carry the reindeer and me across the canyon. "That's it!"

"Do you have a brilliant idea?" Ardee asked hopefully.

"I have an idea. It's too obvious to be brilliant." I would have grinned, but the cold hurt my teeth. Instead, I reached under my coat. The pouch was stiff with cold, and I struggled to open it. Finally, I pulled out the rope and touched the second knot. "Here we go again!"

"Oh, fiddlesticks!" The reindeer stiffened and closed her eyes. "Just tell me when it's over."

The ribbon wind sliced through the purple sky, a ghostly streamer of arctic breath. I tried to hang on to the reindeer's fur, but the wind didn't pick us up together this time. First it sailed under Ardee's belly, looped over her back, sailed under her belly again, and jerked tight as it yanked the reindeer off the ground.

At the same time as Ardee's hooves left the ground, the wind whipped around my chest. Still clinging to the rope, I raised my arms so they wouldn't be trapped when the ribbon wind tightened. Takeoff was sudden, and the wind rose skyward too fast for sightseeing. It did not adjust course to avoid the bulges in the frozen waterfall. I had to be on guard, pushing off the ice wall with my free hand and my feet so I wouldn't smash into the hard mounds. Ardee squealed every time she banged into the ice. Her sharp hooves cut deep when she hit, causing a spray of ice crystals.

The icy specks were so cold they stung my face. I tried tucking my chin, but slivers of ice cut the skin on my cheeks anyway. My first impulse was to swat the bits away. Then I realized that the crystals swarming around my head like angry bees were actually alive. Since Ardee and I had disturbed them, I couldn't justify doing them more harm. I was sure someone was keeping track of such things in Aventurine. How else would the fairies know which fairy-godmothers-in-the-making deserved to return and complete the training?

All such thoughts ceased when the ice creatures fled in a sudden, frantic flurry. Just as the last one flew away, a hairy hand burst through the ice and grabbed my wrist.

7

Fairy Lights

I am hardly a screamer, but *this* made me scream — as loud as I could. Thankfully, the wind stopped instantly, so that I hung suspended against the ice wall instead of having my arm ripped off.

"What's happening!" Ardee shrieked. "Why did we stop? Are we there yet? Oh, I can't look!" The wind had clearly stopped going up with her, too.

The hairy hand was attached to the hairy arm of a monster trapped in the ice. Round eyes glared at me from a misshapen face that was framed by black spikes streaked with silver. The mouth was curled in a sneer, showing yellow teeth. A blood-red coat covered the monster's bulging belly.

It reminded me of another folktale my father used to tell me, about a fur trapper who had been frozen behind a waterfall at the sudden onslaught of winter. He could escape only if he captured a human girl to melt the ice, freeing him as she froze in his place.

My arm had started to freeze in the monster's grip. While my flesh was turning to ice, the ice encasing the monster's arm melted.

I gasped. *I* was the girl! And if I didn't find a way out, I'd be frozen in the waterfall! I still held the magic rope in my free hand. There was one knot left. I was already using the ribbon wind, so the knot couldn't help me. But I didn't dare drop it to grab my Kalis stick. It couldn't smash through tons of ice, and if I survived, I would need the knot later.

"I think I'm going to throw up," Ardee moaned.

I had one thing to offer the monster, the only other thing I had acquired since leaving the Willowood Fairies: the elf's message.

Could an elf have a troll or an ogre for a brother? I didn't know, but I was out of ideas so I delivered the message.

I shouted it, hoping he could hear through the ice. "The elf on the beach wanted me to tell you: 'If the wind goes free, so will we.'"

Instantly, the monster opened his hand and released my wrist. A tingly sensation coursed through my arm as my blood started circulating again, but my joy encompassed much more than my freedom. The first elf had predicted his brother would find me if my path was true.

We had not strayed off the trail.

The ice melted around the elf's brother, forming an alcove. It turned out the second elf wasn't huge or grotesque — the wavy ice had just wildly distorted him. Rounder than his brother, with chubby cheeks, a furrowed brow, and a dour expression, he was also two feet tall.

I remembered my manners. "Thanks for letting go of my arm," I said, still dangling in the air. The magical wind hovered in place, apparently waiting for a cue to start moving again.

"Had to," the elf growled, folding his arms and scowling. "My brother sent you. I didn't want to."

"But you did all the same." I extended my hand. "I can take you to the top of the icefall."

"Why would I want to go there?" he snapped.

"Why would you want to stay here?" I asked, curious.

"Because it's not the top of Dayling Mountain," the elf huffed. "I have no use for Dayling Mountain. No use at all." He did not possess a smidgeon of his brother's lyrical manner or poetic talent.

"Can we go now?" Ardee moaned.

"In a minute." I still had business with the elf. I was a bit put out by his disdain for *my* mountain, but he had let me go and I owed him a favor. I had to repay him or face worse than a few bitter words when the disagreeable little man decided to get even. "Is there anything I can do for you?"

"I can hope, but I won't count on it." Heaving a great sigh, the elf said, "Give that same message to my brother if you see him, which you won't."

"Why won't I?" I asked.

"You're just a child," the elf growled. "Not a bit of sense in your head, or you wouldn't be hanging around here."

I guessed I'd be cranky, too, if I had been frozen on a mountain while my sister lived at the beach. Still, that didn't make it right to be so rude. Since as far as I knew I was under no obligation to stay and take the elf's insults, I tugged on the ribbon wind.

Ardee screeched as the current resumed our superfast ride up the icefall. As soon as we cleared the top of the icefall, the ribbon unwound Ardee and me like toy tops and dropped us in a snowbank. I was glad to be alive and thankful that I wasn't climbing the icefall inch by inch.

"I do not want to ride that scary thing ever again," Ardee complained as she pawed her way out of the deep drift. She shook snow off her antlers and stamped packed ice out of her hooves.

"And what if you were cornered by the wolf with no other way out?" I teased as I peered down at the glacier.

"Okay, maybe then," Ardee admitted. "But not for anything else."

I didn't laugh. Instead, I looked over the edge of the icefall to see how high we were. I inhaled softly when I saw a speck of gray; the wolf was at the base of the ice wall far below.

I was sure the wolf couldn't climb, but with its thick coat of fur, it could easily survive the winter weather on the mountain. When the wolf leapt onto an ice shelf and disappeared, I realized it didn't have to follow in our footsteps to catch us. It could take alternate routes and backtrack to pick up our scent anywhere we had been.

I decided not to tell Ardee that the wolf was still after us. Putting the knotted rope back in my pouch, I looked for the path. I couldn't see it on the ice and drifted snow, but Ardee found it—with her nose.

"Other animals have used this path before," she explained. "It goes this way."

I pulled my hood around my face a bit more and followed the reindeer away from the icefall. The path became a ledge that wound steeply upward with a sharp drop-off on the right. There was just enough room for my boots on the slippery ledge. I inched along, hugging the rocks and moving my feet forward without lifting my boots off the ground, the wind whipping about us. Ardee paused every few minutes to wait for me. She wasn't afraid of falling.

The temperature fell several more degrees, making the air so brittle I could almost hear it crack. Frost formed on my eyelashes, and the sky deepened from violet to dark blue.

"Can you still see?" I shouted to be heard above the wind.

"Yes!" Ardee called back.

I slipped backward, and the reindeer immediately shouted, "Kerka! Are you hurt?"

"Just my pride!" I yelled, grabbing Ardee's back leg to steady myself as I struggled to rise. Her rimmed hoof kept her anchored on the incline.

"Hold on to my tail!" Ardee said when I was back on my feet. "So I can pull you up if you fall."

I hesitated. If I stumbled and fell off the cliff, I might drag her over, too.

"Please," Ardee pleaded. "It won't hurt. Besides, if you fall, I'd rather die with you than lose you."

I believed her and moved closer, clutching her

short tail with both hands. "You're very brave, Ardee."

"No, I'm sure-footed, and I don't want anything to happen to you," Ardee said, bending her head to press on.

With darkness descending and a frigid wind hampering every step, we crept forward like an arctic snail. I had no idea how long the Aventurine night would last. I had to find Biba's voice before the sun rose. There would be no do-overs.

We could fly the remaining length of the narrow ledge if I touched the third knot. However, using it to lessen the hardship and save time didn't seem wise. Although we were moving slowly, we were moving forward. I decided to keep the knot for a situation we couldn't handle without help.

A moment later, my feet slipped out from under me and I fell on my knees. Ardee turned and a chunk of snow-covered rock broke off the ledge. One hoof slipped off.

"Just stay still," Ardee called out. "I'm okay."

I waited until the reindeer got her hoof back on solid ice.

"Can you get up?" Ardee asked.

"I'll try." I got onto my knees, but when I tried to

stand, my boots slid out from under me again. "The ice is too slick!"

Ardee held out one of her back hooves to me. "Hold on to me, then," she said. "I'll pull you until we find a bare spot."

Being dragged along an ice shelf holding on to a reindeer's hoof is not fun. My arms began to ache and Ardee's hooves sprayed chips of ice as she walked. I couldn't protect my face, but I kept my eyes closed. Just when my mittens began to slip off Ardee's hoof, the path took a sharp left turn into a ravine.

"You can let go now," Ardee said.

I collapsed onto bare rocky ground and rolled over, taking a minute to catch my breath. High rock walls on both sides of the ravine shielded us from the wind and blowing snow. The sky overhead was a darker shade of blue laced with faint puffs of light. I blinked, but my eyes weren't playing tricks. The tiny puffs really did appear here and there.

Ardee looked down at me. "Are you okay?"

"Fine," I said, getting to my feet. My legs ached from the climb, but we didn't have time to rest. It would be night soon.

The trail through the protected niche was still

icy, and I stayed behind Ardee, clinging to her tail as we walked ever upward. When the reindeer paused to dig in a pile of snow, I didn't argue. My knees were a little shaky and I needed the break.

"What are you doing?" I asked.

"I need a snack." The reindeer looked back. "You're not going to yell at me, are you?"

"No!" I shook my head. "You've earned a treat, but there's no grass up here."

"I know," Ardee said. "I like reindeer moss just as much."

I watched, fascinated, as she plunged her muzzle into the snow. When she lifted her head, she had a mouthful of gray lichen. "It's very dry," she said after the third bite. "Can we use more magic water now?"

I was thirsty, too, but the pouches weren't insulated. "The pods might be frozen."

"They might not," Ardee said, chewing another wad of lichen.

"Let's find out." I rubbed my hands together under the coat to warm my stiff fingers before I opened my backpack. The water pod was cold, and nothing happened when I poked it. "It's frozen."

"Oh." Ardee swayed from side to side. She quickly added a warning. "But we can't eat snow."

"I know." I sighed, absently rolling the cold pod

between my hands while I mulled over the problem. We had to drink to keep going, but eating ice or snow would lower our body temperatures. That would make us more dehydrated, not less.

"Do you have a brilliant idea yet?" Ardee placed her chin on my chest and begged with her big blue winter eyes. "Please have a brilliant idea."

"I wish it was that easy, Ardee, but—" I inhaled sharply then grinned when I realized the pod wasn't frozen anymore. Friction and body heat had warmed it up in my hands. "No brilliant ideas, but how about an accidental one?"

"Will it make water?" Ardee backed up a step.

Keeping my hands under the coat, I rolled the pod between my palms as fast as I could until it was hot. It began to cool when I held it outside my coat and jabbed it, but when the pod expanded and split open, the water inside was still warm. It tasted as good as sweet tea or hot chocolate sliding down my throat, and the heat radiated from my stomach to warm my whole insides. I gave Ardee a little more than half.

The reindeer drained the pod and burped. "It's a good thing you're so smart."

"The fairies thought of everything, not me," I said.

"Then it's very good you're smart enough to figure out fairy things." Snorting, Ardee turned and began walking.

"We make a good team," I said, trudging after her.

"Yes, we do." She flicked her tail. "Grab on to my tail if it gets slippery again."

The hike up the ravine was easier going than the ledge, but it didn't last. The instant we left the shelter of the rock walls, we were hit by winds and driving snow. Ardee turned broadside, inserting her body between me and the wind so I wouldn't be blown off my feet. Although traces of twilight lingered, we were both blind in the blizzard.

We couldn't see the path to continue on, and we would freeze to death if we didn't keep moving.

I pulled out the rope and touched the last knot.

As though by magic, which it was, the wind obeyed my unspoken command and calmed to a whisper. The swirling snow settled, creating lacy patterns on the rocks. As I looked around to get my bearings, I realized that the third knot had saved us from more than the winter storm. The reindeer and I were standing on a narrow ice bridge that spanned a deep canyon. The bridge was no more than eighteen inches wide. A step to either side and we would have fallen off. The knot had saved our lives.

Shaken by yet another close call, I looked down into the dark chasm. *Did I decide to save the last knot based on intuition, logic, or luck? Did it matter why or how as long as it was the right decision?*

I frowned in thought. Even with great intuition, the best information, and uncanny good luck, no one knew exactly the right thing to do at all times without fail. Everybody made mistakes. The difference was in how each person handled them. My mother always said that insecure people got mad or made excuses or blamed someone else. Stupid people wouldn't even admit there had been a mistake. Smart people learned from their mistakes and with luck made fewer as they went through life.

I *tried* to be smart, but making decisions was complicated. When I had time, I tried to consider all the good and bad things involved. And that was all I or anyone else could expect.

"Fairy lights," Ardee said, her voice filled with wistful longing. "It looks like home."

I looked up. Night had truly fallen while I was deep in thought, but the sky wasn't black.

Shimmering grayish lights with faint tints of blue and green were splashed across diamond-studded dark blue velvet. Sprays of silver exploded behind starbursts of blue while waves of gray rippled underneath. Tendrils of green lightning flashed, sputtered out, and then flashed again. The aurora borealis in Finland's Arctic skies had more dazzling colors, but otherwise they looked the same. My mother called the northern lights a cosmic magic show, created by the universe to preserve the sense of wonder too many children lose when they grow up.

"It looks like my home, too," I said, blinking back a tear. I missed my mother, my father, my sisters, and the carefree days of my childhood. A tear froze on my cheek, and I brushed it away. I couldn't complete the tasks ahead if I was a lump of blubbering mush.

"We're almost to the top!" Ardee exclaimed, swishing her tail with excitement.

A natural bridge connected the ravine to the base of the mountain peak. I couldn't tell if the bridge was made of rock or just ice covered with snow. Queen Patchouli had sent me here so I was pretty sure the suspended path would hold our weight. Still, for a second, I wondered if I had used the third knot too soon.

"Is something wrong?" Ardee asked.

"No." I didn't want to scare her. We had to cross the bridge to reach the mountain peak. I pointed to where the bridge path widened several feet farther out. "Let's move to safer footing."

The reindeer pranced forward, secure on the ice pack. I put the wind rope back in its pouch and followed at a more sedate pace. Fearful of stepping on a weak spot that might break off, I placed my boots in Ardee's hoofprints and held my breath. I paused where the bridge widened to three feet across, captivated by the astounding view.

Illuminated by the fairy lights overhead, we could see Aventurine below us. A layer of daylight blanketed the ground under the darkness. I could see the ridge of the boulder wall by the beach, across the Glass Lake to the shores of the Willowood and beyond, to the lilacs by the glass wall and the Orchards of Allfruit. I thought I spotted the green branches of Birdie's Glimmer Tree just before the terrain faded into a hazy horizon, but then I realized I couldn't possibly see that far. The landmarks were the handiwork of a fairy's whim, drawn from my memory and imagination.

"What's that tall pointy thing?" Ardee was looking at the view on the other side of the bridge.

I turned, expecting to see parts of Aventurine I hadn't visited yet. I gasped when I saw the waking world stretching to another hazy horizon. Far to one side, the green domes of the Helsinki Cathedral and the tall Olympic Tower stood out like toys placed on a paper map of the world. I glanced over the Eiffel Tower, one of Aunt Tuula's favorite places, across the whitecaps on the Atlantic Ocean to the Statue of Liberty in New York Harbor. Ardee was staring at New York City.

"That's the Empire State Building," I said. "It was the tallest building in the waking world for a long, long time."

"But it's not as tall as *your* mountain," the reindeer said.

I smiled as I shifted my gaze back to Aventurine, amazed by the fairies' artistry. Two worlds seen from a mountaintop was a masterpiece. But I couldn't stop and stare any longer. I urged Ardee to move on and quickened my own pace. I was getting tired, but I didn't want to fall behind.

The wings came out of nowhere. The huge bird swooped down on us from the dark blue sky. I ducked, but it flew so close, its talons snagged my hair. I staggered toward the edge of the bridge.

"No!" I shouted and grabbed for Ardee. She clamped on to the back of my coat with her teeth and pulled back. She was stronger than the bird and kept me from falling off. The bird screeched as it flew off. I landed in a sitting position under Ardee's nose, but I wasn't out of danger. The bird flew in a wide arc and started back.

"Duck!" I drew up my knees and covered my head with my arms.

Ardee let go of my coat and stood her ground. The white bird flew straight at us. At the last second, Ardee rattled her antlers and gave a warning cry that sounded like a foghorn! The bird decided she didn't want to tangle with Ardee and whooshed over us.

"What was that?" I asked as I watched the bird disappear into the darkening sky.

"A snowy owl," the reindeer said. "It must be guarding something."

"How do you know?" I asked.

"I don't know," Ardee said. "Some answers just seem to be in my head. But I don't have the answers to what I really want."

"I think a lot of people feel that way," I said. I stood up and rocked back on my heels, shaking.

I took a deep breath. So far, Queen Patchouli's

faith in my abilities wasn't misplaced. The last leg of my ascent to the peak was within sight, at the far end of the ice bridge. I had come a long way and had endured much.

With Ardee's help, I reminded myself. I let her take the lead across the rest of the bridge.

8

The Kalistonia Fairies

My legs buckled when we stepped off the ice bridge. I fell against a large boulder and sank to my knees, too cold and exhausted to go on.

Ardee nosed me in the side and gently pawed me with her hoof. Her voice shook with urgency. "Don't lie down, Kerka."

"I'm too tired to walk another step." My words were slurred and hard to hear. I was even too tired to talk. I leaned my head against the rock and closed my eyes.

"Get up." Ardee nudged me harder. "You have a mission. Important things to do, you said."

"I have to rest," I insisted. "*Then* I'll go do important things."

"Reindeer that fall down to rest never get up,"

Ardee said firmly. "They freeze or get eaten by wolves."

Wolf? Fear-induced adrenaline brought me out of my stupor. I shook my head to clear my brain, but I couldn't shake the weariness in my bones and muscles. Still, I couldn't ignore Ardee's warning.

Grabbing the reindeer's long hair, I pulled myself up. My legs wobbled like spaghetti, and I couldn't feel my feet. Leaning across Ardee's back, I rubbed my hands and stamped my boots to quicken the flow of blood through my body, but I struggled to keep my eyes open.

"If I don't rest soon, I won't have the strength to finish my quest," I explained. "We have to stop when we find shelter."

"A shelter where the wolf can't go," Ardee said.

"Is it nearby?" I gasped, feeling foolish for trying to hide the predator's pursuit. The reindeer would catch the wolf's scent long before I saw or heard it.

"No, but it's coming," Ardee said.

The fairy lights cast a flickering glow over the path as it wound through crevices in the rocky terrain. We were no longer in danger of falling off a cliff, but sleep was a constant temptation. Using Ardee as a crutch, I dragged one foot after the other and scanned dark recesses in the mountainside, looking for a haven from the brutal cold. We found a few caves, but they were too narrow to enter or were shallow dead ends. I finally nodded off for a few seconds and heard a soft voice.

"This way . . ."

Startled, I awoke and quickly glanced around, as though the dreamed words were real and not a whisper of the wind. Notches and cave openings looked like slices of night behind the dancing fairy lights. My eyes focused on a sliver of black set deeper into the rock. The opening wasn't wide enough for me or a reindeer with antlers to slip through, but I was drawn to it anyway.

"There." I let go of the reindeer to investigate. Aided by the glimmering lights, I reached the fissure in the rock without mishap. A massive boulder camouflaged a large cave entrance, and Ardee hung back when I stepped inside. The darkness was so black I couldn't see my hand. "We'll be safe here," I told the reindeer.

"It's too dark," Ardee protested. She was still standing outside. "I'm afraid of the dark."

"That's why it's safe," I explained, trying not to lose patience. "It doesn't look like a cave from the path, and the darkness will keep other creatures out."

"Maybe, I guess." Ardee set one hoof inside, her

resolve faltering. "I wouldn't come in if you weren't making me." After thinking about it a few more seconds, Ardee gave in. "Hold on to me and don't let go. I don't want to get lost."

Twining my fingers in Ardee's neck hair, I used the lessons I had learned in the dark woods and stretched out my other arm. Taking tiny steps and feeling my way, I avoided running into the rock walls. The cramped passageway didn't lead directly into a larger cavern. We had to turn at every wall, first left, then right, then left again. There wasn't yet room to lie down comfortably so we kept going. As we walked deeper into the mountain, a dim yellow-green glow began to filter through the darkness.

Ardee stopped suddenly, sitting back on her haunches and stubbornly refusing to move. "A troll must live down here . . . or maybe something worse."

"Do you smell something, Ardee?" If a dangerous being was lurking in the rocks, I wanted to know. If not, I had to calm the reindeer's jittery nerves so she didn't bolt out of the cave. I could never catch her, but the wolf would.

Raising her muzzle, Ardee sniffed. Her tense muscles

relaxed under my hand. "Nothing stinky-bad."

Relieved, I continued walking. "I bet the glow comes from lichen."

"There's no such thing as light-up lichen," Ardee scoffed. Distracted by my theory, she walked with me.

"We have lots of glowing life forms in the waking world," I argued. "Fireflies, glow worms, mushrooms, and deep sea jellyfish, for instance. Even wolf eyes glow in the dark. I'm sure Aventurine has such things, too. Probably more, because of the amount of magic here."

Around the next curve, the passageway opened into a small circular cave with a domed ceiling. Everything in the cave glowed, from clusters of small yellow bell-shaped flowers on large rocks to giant moths with green wings. Transparent crystal stalactites hung down from the ceiling over matching stalagmites that reached up from the floor. Large, glowing white worms ducked in and out of holes in the rock walls, causing an oddly soothing strobe effect.

Ignoring the glorious sight, Ardee sniffed a wide

patch of thick brown moss and tried a small nibble. She spit it out. "It tastes awful, but it's soft. You can sleep on it."

"Good." Yawning, I sat down. I shifted the pouches so I wouldn't squash them and took my Kalis stick out of my backpack. I knew I would feel more secure sleeping with it in my hand.

"The cave creatures probably don't like that disgusting sour moss, either," Ardee added as she settled on the hard floor beside the spongy lichen mat. "But I can't be one hundred percent positive. Some porcupines eat pine needles, and I can't stand them."

I didn't like the idea of hungry creepy crawlies squirming around me munching moss, but that wasn't my biggest concern. Despite my exhaustion, I was afraid to fall asleep. What if I didn't wake up in time?

"Lie close to me," Ardee said. "I'll keep you warm."

"Thanks, but I'm worried I'll oversleep." On camping trips in Finland, I always woke up at the first light of dawn, but there was no sunlight inside the cave and I was far more tired than I had ever been in my life.

"Reindeer are light sleepers," Ardee said.

"Waking up at every little thing is one of our best defenses. When do you want to get up?"

I couldn't answer. The sun rose in Aventurine on a whim, not on a schedule. I told Ardee the first thing that popped into my mind and hoped my intuitive answer was correct. "In three hours."

"I'll stay alert for the wolf," Ardee said, "and I'll wake you in . . ."

Snuggling against Ardee's warm hide, I was sound asleep before she finished her sentence.

I woke up suddenly, startled by a metallic whine.

"What's that?" Ardee whispered.

"I don't know." Tightening my grip on my Kalis stick, I waited for my eyes to adjust to the glowing creature-lights. Behind a bank of tall stalagmites, another passageway led off the small room. I rose and quietly crept toward it.

"Where are you going?" Ardee hissed as she stood up.

I looked back and held my fingers to my lips. Then I motioned for the reindeer to stay put and wait. Ardee didn't pay any attention; she followed me into an arched tunnel and I didn't have the heart to stop her.

The yellow flowers grew in clumps among colonies of worms on the walls, shining light for us to see by. As we walked deeper into the mountain, the metallic sounds grew louder, the tunnel widened, the glowing creatures were bigger, and the light glowed brighter. A blue substance that looked like mercury filled hollows and cracks in the big flat rocks that lined the walls. Splotches of the blue liquid moved from one pool to another at a languid pace, as if it were alive. Other rocks were covered with puffs of glowing pink lichen.

At the end of the tunnel was what looked like a huge cavern; a faint sound came from it, like vibrating chimes or metal drums. I ducked behind a tall boulder at the edge of the opening, wary of any unforeseen danger beyond. Ardee stood behind me, peeking out.

"I'm hungry," she said.

"Shh," I responded. "Not now."

I looked over just in time to see her sniff a glowing pink puff on the boulder and recoil. "It bit me!" she yelped, wiggling her stung nose as though she had to sneeze.

"Shhhh!" I whispered loudly and glared. "Don't eat anything. You could make yourself sick. Or maybe even eat something that's a some*one*. Just wait here. Please. And I mean it this time."

The reindeer sighed and nodded. "Okay, but if you find any food—"

"I'll bring it back," I promised.

Once Ardee was settled, I gave the cave my complete attention. I couldn't see much from my hiding place, but I realized that the metallic sound had many parts, like musical instruments in an orchestra. A blast of hot air hit the back of my neck. I jumped slightly, swallowing a squeal. I began to sweat under my heavy coat and quickly discovered the heat source in the wall behind me: orange fungus that looked like the tops of pumpkins without stems. Every few seconds, the orange segments burst open and blew out heated air. A quick scan confirmed that thousands of the furnace plants—or maybe they were furnace animals—lived in the rocky walls.

The cavern was as bright and as warm as a summer day. Dropping my coat, I scurried toward the next boulder with my Kalis stick in hand. The astonishing beauty of the underground wonderland didn't make an impact until I completely cleared the corridor. Awestruck, I stopped to gawk.

Light from many species of luminescent creatures reflected off a network of crystal stalactites and stalagmites. The cavern walls were honeycombed with alcoves, all of them alight in brilliant colors. Fairies dressed in earth tones and watery hues danced Kalis on one side, their sticks every shade of the rainbow. Ordinary flowering plants, vines, and grasses grew everywhere: on the ground, between the rocks, and around crystal structures. A gentle stream of water flowed off a high ledge into a pool. Roly-poly animals covered in artichoke-like scales bounced on a bed of silver leaves.

I remembered Queen Patchouli's second piece of advice: Look for the Kalistonia Fairies. Maybe my goal was closer than I realized. At the very least, the Kalistonia Fairies were a marker on the path to find Biba's voice. I looked more closely at the fairies in the cavern.

Fairy ages are impossible to pinpoint, but most of the girls looked like teenagers. They all had simple swirling designs on their foreheads and arms. I couldn't tell if they were painted on or marks they were born with. Some of the fairies' clothes sparkled with mica or gemstones. Instead of the long, flowing dresses of the Willowood Fairies, these fairies wore clothes that were easy to perform the Kalis moves in. They all wore their hair in braids, either hanging down or pinned up, some in intricate patterns.

Their Kalis sticks were different lengths and

colors, and the sticks made different sounds as they whistled through the air. The cathedral cavern reverberated with whirs, whistles, and chimes. The longest sticks made a sound like tumbling crystal beads.

Although the fairies were moving with flawless grace and fluidity, jumping higher and spinning faster than I'd seen before, I recognized several of the movements. They were variations of the basic Kalis steps my mother had taught me. A fairy dressed in deep brown stood on the tip of a stalagmite. Balanced on one foot, she bent her knee and sprang straight up. Reaching for the high ceiling with her Kalis stick, she brought her legs together and twisted like a corkscrew as she settled to the ground.

A younger fairy stood among toadstools, practicing the movement my mother called Stroking the Water Horse's Mane. The dancer in smoky gray held her left arm out to the side. Holding her lavender Kalis stick in her right hand, she swept her right arm down to the left over the imaginary crest of a horse's neck and then looped it up and back. Repeating the movement over and over again, she practiced to achieve perfection and only stopped once. She stared at her short Kalis stick a moment and then resumed the same routine.

Other fairies danced in pairs, leaping in unison or mirroring each other's moves. Despite the distance from my spying spot, I could see the nuance in each movement. Mesmerized, I watched a girl who rounded herself into a ball. She held the position for three heartbeats and then sprang from the floor, throwing her arms and legs out like an unfolding flower. I felt the snap and collapse of her slim body as she performed the X Sweep. On the sixth unfolding, she launched herself into the air and drifted upward like a dandelion seed carried on the breeze.

A series of sharp, staccato whacks followed by a *thwang* rose above the sounds of the dancing fairies' sticks. I peeked around the other side of the boulder. Here, older fairies danced in pairs amid crystals and gigantic ferns.

These fairies were dressed similarly to the younger ones, except their wings were held tight against their backs with two strips of fabric that crossed over their chests and around their backs. Leaping from jagged rock to pointed stalagmite, they twisted and turned with a fury I had never associated with fairies. The swirling designs on their foreheads and arms were far more complex than those on the younger fairies. Many had the patterns on their calves and ankles as well. Their Kalis sticks were longer, some measuring over four feet, and I didn't recognize a single move as I watched.

I was sure that the young dancers and Kalis masters had to be the Kalistonia Fairies Queen Patchouli mentioned, but I needed to be sure. Squaring my shoulders, I stepped out of hiding. I held my small orange Kalis stick pointing down lest my intentions be mistaken as unfriendly. As I raised my empty hand to get someone's attention, all the fairies in the cavern stopped moving.

"Oh, please, don't stop," I cried, without even meaning to.

All the fairies lowered their Kalis sticks and bowed, their gazes turned upward.

I stared, speechless.

A beautiful, statuesque fairy looked down from a crystal tower thirty feet above. Stepping off, she floated down to the floor without using the small wings on her back at all. The scallops of her pale tunic fell below the tops of soft brown high boots tied with crisscrossed thongs. Holding a five-foot golden-white Kalis stick, she glided across the floor and stopped a few feet away from me. Her heart-shaped face reminded me of Aunt Tuula's, with laugh lines at the corners of her eyes and mouth and a nose that crinkled when she smiled. Her long braids were twined around her head in a crown style similar to Aunt Tuula's as well.

Before I could ask the question poised on my tongue, the fairy flicked her Kalis stick. The stick sparkled as it telescoped down to eighteen inches. Then, bowing in a sweeping gesture of honorable welcome, she said: "I am Mangi, Queen of the Kalistonia Fairies. We have been waiting for you."

"Waiting for me?" I asked, stunned.

"The Kalistonia Fairies teach all fairy-godmothers-in-the-making from the Pax Lineage," Queen Mangi said. "I've been expecting you for some time now, Kerka."

I shouldn't have been surprised that Queen Mangi knew I had come to Aventurine. One of my mother's daughters had to begin fairy godmother training or our family's branch of the Pax Lineage would be banished from the fairy world.

The fairy queen looked past me. "You can come out now, Ardee," she said, raising an eyebrow when the reindeer made no move to obey.

"It's okay, Ardee," I said, talking over my shoulder and making a come-here gesture behind my back.

"She's a bit shy," the queen observed.

"A bit," I agreed. Something else puzzled me, though. "How did you know the reindeer's name?"

"I heard it through the grapevine," the queen answered with a twinkle in her eye.

"Do grapevines grow underground through the whole mountain?" I asked.

"They grow wherever we need them," Queen Mangi said.

I wanted to know more, but I didn't want to be nosy. I glanced back and caught Ardee peeking around the boulder. She quickly ducked back, but I could see the tips of her antlers. So could the curious young dancers who had come closer. They pointed and giggled.

"You must be hungry after your long journey," Queen Mangi said, smiling ever so slightly when the reindeer peeked out again.

"I have food." I touched the pouch. "The Willowood Fairies were very generous, but they didn't give me anything for a reindeer."

Ardee walked up and stopped behind me.

"We have reindeer provisions," Queen Mangi said, as though reindeer visited the Kalistonia Fairies all the time. "Despite the shortness of time, it is important that I show you our realm. It should help you to understand some of your Pax Lineage."

"Are you sure it is okay?" I asked.

"Not just okay, but necessary," Queen Mangi

answered. "You'll see why. And you should have some time to eat when we're done."

"But I'm hungry right *now*," Ardee said, planting her feet.

"Shh!" I nudged the reindeer with my elbow. Hunger gnawed at my stomach, too, but I'd rather suffer than be rude.

"Of course you're hungry," Queen Mangi said graciously. "Reindeer eat twelve pounds of fodder a day, and you've had a very tough day."

"A very, very tough day," the reindeer agreed.

Queen Mangi hid another amused smile. "We'll look for a good snack along the way. Just remember that most of the plants in these caverns are not food."

"Puffy pink things aren't friendly." Ardee shook her antlers and curled her upper lip. "They bite."

"Perhaps puffy pink things don't like to be eaten," Queen Mangi suggested, winking at me. She stepped onto a path of smooth round stones inlaid with precious gems.

Ardee stamped her hoof but followed anyway.

"Please stay on the pathway," Queen Mangi said. "We don't want to trample anyone."

The path wandered between tall crystal stalagmites, curving this way and that and sometimes looping back. The pattern seemed random at first. Then

I noticed that all the ceiling stalactites had a matching floor stalagmite. Not a single structure had been removed, chiseled, or chipped. The paved pathway had been built around them.

The queen paused in a large alcove where an underground spring of clear mountain water bubbled up into a crystal pool. Spotted brown frogs sat among reeds or floated on lily pads. Silver and black moths perched on gray-green lichen shaped like fans.

"Please, quench your thirst." Queen Mangi swept her hand toward the pool. "Pod water gets stale after awhile."

Ardee plunged her muzzle into the pool and sucked in water with a loud slurping sound. No one seemed to mind. I drank from my cupped hand, wishing I could slurp. The spring water tasted like mountain air: cold, crisp, and clean. When we were full, Ardee eyed a patch of clover.

"May I eat them?" she asked the queen in a voice filled with longing.

A chattering noise, like tiny squirrels scolding an intruder, came from the clovers.

"Thank you for asking before eating," the queen told Ardee. "The clovers tell me that a delicious variety of reindeer moss grows nearby. Why don't you eat some and tell me if that's true, Ardee."

"Okay!" Ardee's ears perked forward, and she stopped moping. "How far is it?"

"It's not far. The Kalis stick nursery is just ahead." The queen swept away down the path, and I jogged to catch up.

"Did you say nursery? Are Kalis sticks *born*?" I had assumed fairies *made* my precious orange stick.

"In a way," Queen Mangi said. "You'll see."

9

In the Caves of Kalistonia

I don't like it when people avoid answering a question they intend to answer later, but I kept quiet and just followed Queen Mangi.

The path exited the crystal maze and went into a large garden. Moss, mushrooms, and fungi grew on rocks and under small fig trees with twisted branches. Blackberry vines grew in straight lines toward the ceiling instead of in tangles. They bent when a fairy wanted berries that were too high to reach. Young fairies carried water in hollowed-out gourds to plants that weren't rooted near one of the springs. An older fairy clipped dead leaves and buried them to replenish the ground. Insects and small creatures that I recognized—and many I didn't—were everywhere I looked.

"The garden exists in a harmonious cycle of life,

and everything has a sense of purpose," Queen Mangi told us. "Flies consider it an honor to be eaten by a lizard, and bees make more honey than they use. Glow worms clean harmful microbes off the rocks, and pink puffs pump nutrients into the soil through hollow roots."

"And no one ever fights?" I was amazed.

"Not very often," Queen Mangi said. "Raspberries get huffy if they're picked before they're ripe."

Ardee stopped suddenly, sniffing the air. "I smell reindeer moss."

We turned into a wide corridor filled with snowdrifts, where the temperature dropped suddenly. No furnace creatures lived in the walls here, and snowflakes fell through a hole in the ceiling a hundred feet up.

"You may eat anything you find under the snow," Queen Mangi told Ardee. "We'll be back this way soon."

"Thank you," Ardee said, pawing the drifts.

I looked back as we continued down the corridor and caught Ardee watching us. She looked slightly worried, but then she lowered her head to eat. I knew she'd be all right until we came back. Nothing in the fairy caves would harm her.

Skip-walking to keep up with the queen, I kept my eyes on the golden glow pouring through the archway at the end of the corridor. My fingers tingled where they touched my Kalis stick. The vibration grew stronger as we drew closer to the archway. We passed through it into the warmth and light, and I came to an abrupt halt and stared.

The ceiling was covered with glowing crystals that looked like icicles. They lit up the entire cavern. Specks of mica twinkled on the walls.

Suddenly Ardee's voice came from behind me and I felt her warm breath on my neck. "I wanted to see, too," the reindeer said.

"Is it okay?" I asked Queen Mangi.

"I'm delighted she wants to join us," the queen said. "This way, please."

A forest of small willow saplings filled most of the space. There were also rocks, more glowing critters, small waterfalls, and a few large crystal stalactite-stalagmite pairs scattered throughout the cavern. Instead of cutting through the rows of young trees, the mosaic stone path hugged the wall.

"These are Kalistonian willows," Queen Mangi said. "Your Kalis stick grew up here, Kerka."

My stick hummed in my hand.

Queen Mangi added, "We don't cut down Kalistonian willows for Kalis sticks, Kerka. Here, I'll show you." She glanced over the rows of young trees. "Would anyone like to volunteer?"

All the four-foot saplings shook their branches. Queen Mangi chose the one nearest the path. Kneeling, she gently removed the soil from around the roots and lifted the tree out of the ground. Cupping the roots, she held the small tree up so I could see.

Roots, branches, and bark were being absorbed back into the tree's slim trunk. Then the trunk telescoped down to twelve inches, the same size as my Kalis stick.

"Thank you," Queen Mangi told the tree. "But you haven't been chosen yet, so I'll have to put you back."

Roots, branches, and bark sprouted in an instant, and the queen put the small tree back into the ground. She patted the soil around the roots and brushed the dirt off her hands when she stood up.

I glanced at the sapling, then at Queen Mangi's sparkling golden-white stick. "Does your stick get big because it's still a live tree? Why doesn't my stick grow? Is it sick? Did I do something wrong?"

"Patience, Kerka. All your questions will be

answered," Queen Mangi said calmly, then added, "when you need the answers."

"Is there something wrong with asking questions?" I asked, since so many of my questions seemed to be put off.

"I didn't say I wasn't going to answer your questions, Kerka," the queen pointed out. "I just told you that the answers would come when the time was right."

I nodded, and we continued walking around the nursery forest to the far end of the cavern.

"Here is where Kalistonian willows become Kalis sticks," the queen said, gesturing toward a gigantic pair of crystal towers that stood by the cave wall, about ten feet apart.

Water seeped out of the rock wall and trickled down into a pool lined with moss and ringed with pink puffs, ferns, and water lilies. Heat from the furnace creatures in the lower wall created a mist above the pool. Together, the towers and mist refracted the light to create a huge rainbow over the pool. Large vines grew up the rock wall. Two of them hung down over the pool, holding two small Kalis sticks suspended in the rainbow mist.

"The rainbow chooses what color each Kalis

stick will be," Queen Mangi explained. "No two Kalis sticks are the exact same color, and the rainbow knows which variations have not been assigned."

"How many Kalis sticks are there?" I asked the question without thinking. But clearly this was the right time for asking that question, because the queen answered.

"Thousands since the beginning of time, but the rainbow has a million different hues," Queen Mangi replied. "Another Kalis stick may appear to be the same orange color as yours, but it's not."

"Who decides what color we get?" I asked.

"After the sticks are colored, the Kalistonia Fairies decide which stick belongs to which young fairy or girl. Sometimes mothers choose for their daughters." A shadow of sadness passed over the queen's calm face.

"Did my mother choose our sticks?" I asked. Ardee pressed closer, as though she knew I needed support.

"Yes, Kerka, she did," Queen Mangi answered, looking into my eyes.

I pictured my mother standing in this same spot just over a year ago, when our Kalis sticks were removed from the rainbow mist. She had decided that I was orange, Biba was blue, and Rona was green. I felt my chest tightening and pushed the sadness away. Ardee moved off as if she'd been pushed, too. The queen's gaze shifted back to the rainbow, and she gave the smallest sigh.

"Aunt Tuula said grown-up fairy godmothers can only come to Aventurine under very special circumstances," I said, changing the topic.

"That's true," the queen said, nodding. "The bond between a girl and her Kalis stick lasts forever. What could be more special than choosing the talisman and most prized possession of your daughter's entire existence?"

"Nothing," I answered.

"Not in the Pax Lineage," Queen Mangi agreed. "After Britta chose the Three Queens to be the talisman for you and your sisters, the engraver inscribed your sticks: *D* for Dayling, *H* for Hourling, and *Y* for Yearling."

I thought about my sisters and how much this knowledge would mean to them. "Do all Pax Lineage fairy-godmothers-in-the-making get to see the nursery?"

"Most, not all," the queen said, turning. "Time grows short, Kerka, and there is more to see." She glided back through the cavern on the stone path.

Ardee grabbed another mouthful of reindeer

moss as we sped down the cold corridor. She was still chewing when the queen led us into another small chamber. The walls were covered with crystals.

Light glinted off the crystals in beams that intersected at odd angles. It made me feel off balance, like being in a fun house full of mirrors. Ardee wouldn't step inside at all.

The queen faced Ardee and me. "Pax Lineage girls learn the basic Kalis movements from their mothers or another family member in the waking world," Queen Mangi began. "Once a Pax Lineage girl has mastered the basics, she comes to Aventurine to learn advanced techniques. Fully understanding the magic of the dance, its meaning, and its impact on the world is part of becoming a full-fledged fairy godmother."

I bit my lip. Queen Mangi knew that my mother had died before she could teach us the last basic Kalis movement. With Biba still in Finland and Rona too busy to dance anything except ballet, Aunt Tuula hadn't continued my training when I arrived in New York. I decided not to mention it.

"The next phase of training takes place here in the Crystal Chamber," the queen said.

"The trainee is left alone in the chamber with her Kalis stick, to wait for . . . whatever may happen,"

Queen Mangi said. "Every girl reacts differently. Some emerge feeling a great peace within themselves after the experience. Others become filled with self-doubt. Still others are terrified. Human girls who feel this way never return to Aventurine. A fairy girl leaves our caves and finds another fairy tribe to be a part of."

"Why? How?" I asked.

"We are all torn by opposing aspects of our inner selves, Kerka." Queen Mangi gave me some examples. "When facing an enemy, you can surrender or fight. If you surrender, you can give up or run. Do you fight with wits or weapons? When wronged, do you hold a grudge or forgive? Do you help or turn away when aiding another might harm you?"

All *of those decisions could be right or wrong depending on the circumstances*, I thought.

"The crystals in the chamber reach into the core of each girl," the queen continued, "and show her the most important elements of her personality, forcing her to confront them. The Crystal Chamber is only the beginning of the process. When a fairy godmother or a fairy finally reconciles the impulses within, her emotions are balanced and she achieves the Peace of Opposites. For some, understanding comes quickly. Others struggle for a lifetime. But that is why the girls of the Pax Lineage and the tribe of Kalistonia Fairies are forever connected."

I nodded, trying to look as though I knew what she was talking about. In truth, I wasn't at all sure why such a process was necessary.

"Kalis cannot be mastered until you make peace with yourself. Someone who is unsure of themselves can be more easily tricked by an opponent than someone with a clear head."

The explanation made sense, but it didn't calm my own fears. My future as a fairy godmother depended on whether or not I successfully found Biba's voice. I couldn't afford to make a mistake. That fact alone made me doubt my abilities and question my instincts.

"Do I have to go into the Crystal Chamber now?" I asked.

"You haven't mastered all the basic Kalis movements. You haven't even learned the last one," Queen Mangi said, her face completely still. My feelings must have shown on my face because the queen softened her tone. "Besides, there's no time, and if you succeed, there may be no need." In nearly a whisper she added, "Though it would be the first time."

Before I could ask another question, Queen Mangi swept away and led us back into the main cavern. We passed a group of young girl fairies practicing basic Kalis steps on the tops of large toadstools. Queen Mangi stopped at the first garden and watched the older girls perform their more elaborate routines for a minute. Then she selected a pair to come down off their crystal spires and join us.

"Fairy godmothers aren't effective unless they can empathize, and anticipate the feelings, desires, and actions of those they are helping," Queen Mangi explained. "The OneTwoOne Dance teaches partners to feel each other's moves and intentions. Pink Agate and Obsidian have almost achieved perfect harmony." The queen glanced at the waiting fairies. "Please, demonstrate."

I watched, amazed at the dancers' precision. There was no hesitation as they slipped flawlessly from one movement to the next. With both sticks raised, they each executed a Tornado Spin in place and stopped at exactly the same instant. When it looked like both girls would flip their sticks outward to Peek from Behind the High Grass, one of the girls drove the tip of her stick straight toward the other. The second girl was not caught off guard. Anticipating the move, she switched to Stroking the Water Horse's Mane and flipped the first girl's stick aside. The first girl was ready, and gracefully spun with the movement. They ended facing each other with their Kalis sticks crossed.

I applauded. "That looked perfect!"

Smiling, Queen Mangi bowed to the girls. "It *was* perfect."

Both fairies grinned with pride and delight. Their Kalis sticks began to glow and then grew two inches longer.

"They *do* grow!" I exclaimed. "Why didn't you tell me?"

Queen Mangi laughed. "Sometimes it's better to see something than to hear about it. All Kalis sticks are the same when they are first given. They grow and become more powerful as their fairy godmother partners become more accomplished.

"Kalistonia Fairies and Pax fairy godmothers also perform Kalis as a dance and combat technique," Queen Mangi added.

"*Combat?*" The concept of fighting fairy godmothers went against everything I thought I knew.

"Warriors sometimes need to defend those who can't defend themselves," Queen Mangi said.

There were times when I practiced—leaping, spinning, and slashing air—that I felt a burst of energy. It made me feel as though I could take on anything and win. "I didn't know I was *supposed* to be learning to fight."

"You won't be learning to fight just yet," Queen Mangi said. "Fairy-godmothers-in-the-making are not allowed to use fighting powers until they have achieved perfection in the OneTwoOne Dance and more advanced techniques are mastered. A Kalis stick is not ready to be used as a weapon until then."

"But what if something threatens a fairy-godmother-in-the-making?" I asked, thinking of the wolf.

"A master of Kalis tries to outsmart her foes and only fights after all other options have failed." The queen turned to watch the practicing fairies.

I latched on to the fact that she didn't say I absolutely-under-no-circumstances-whatsoever couldn't use Kalis to save myself. I just had to try everything else first. Relieved, I looked back to the dancing fairies. Now that I knew defense was the goal of the exercises, I could see the fighting skills in all the moves. The leaps, spins, kicks, and pauses were like martial arts, and the longer Kalis sticks could be used as swords or like medieval staffs. The beauty of the dance disguised the power of Kalis as a weapon.

Ardee wasn't as interested in the Kalis dancers as I was. She wandered off to explore on her own, probably looking for food.

"I hope I'm a good fighter," I said.

"I hope you're a better peacemaker," Queen Mangi said.

"Peacemaker?" I blinked.

"Pax is the Latin word for peace," Queen Mangi said. "You are seeking the Peace of Opposites not just for yourself, but also for the opposing forces of the world, big and small."

"I don't get it," I said, speaking honestly.

Queen Mangi looked me in the eye. "Members of the Pax Lineage have the magical ability to bring people together even when their differences aren't obvious or seem impossible to reconcile. The task may be as simple as settling an argument between friends or as complicated as negotiating a truce in a war. You may even help someone forgive and forget an injustice."

"If the people I'm trying to help don't know what they need, how will I?" I asked.

"If you master the wind, you will be learning to read what people are feeling," Queen Mangi said. "Both only *seem* elusive. Eventually, you should be able to bring harmony to those in need, just as Kalis is teaching you to bring harmony to yourself."

"Is that what Aunt Tuula does?" I asked.

"Yes." Queen Mangi smiled. "Your aunt calms many fears and creates much goodwill on her travels through the waking world. Your mother brought neighbors together and kept harmony in your whole town. She raised three daughters who rarely argue or squabble."

Not right now, I thought.

"There is something I must tell you, Kerka," Queen Mangi said. "Since you had not learned all the basics of Kalis, I was unsure that you could preserve your family's heritage and place in Aventurine."

My heart sank.

"I was wrong," Queen Mangi continued. "You created a true link with Ardee, and you made the perilous journey from the Glass Lake to this cave. Your intuition and natural abilities are much stronger than I had thought."

My heart lifted, and I asked, "So what should I do now?"

"You must not leave just yet," Queen Mangi said. "There are other things you need to know, things that will improve your chances. I promise you, the Aventurine sun will not begin to rise until after you leave the caves of Kalistonia."

"How do you know?" I was curious.

"Dancing Kalis raises power. The more who dance and the more accomplished the dancers, the more power is raised. Here in Aventurine, with almost all of my fairies dancing, we raise enough power to control time," Queen Mangi said. "Right now, my fairies are dancing to hold the sun back until you are ready to go." Picking up her Kalis stick, the queen motioned for me to follow.

I was blown away by what the queen had said. I looked around to say something to Ardee but she wasn't there. I felt a wave of worry. "Where's Ardee?" I asked. I couldn't let anything happen to her; she needed me.

"She'll be fine until you get back, I promise," Queen Mangi said. She waved over a young fairy. "Take a basket of dried fruit and grass to the cavern entrance."

"And tell her I'll be there soon," I added.

10

Showdown

The fairy nodded and sped off. Queen Mangi led me to a spot between tall stalagmites. No other fairies were in sight. She began another lecture, but I didn't complain.

"A Pax Lineage fairy godmother must have discipline, self-assurance, and wisdom to be a keeper of the peace," Queen Mangi said. "You must also have the power to implement your good works."

"Magic," I said. "Birdie has the power to heal the green world with her family's Singing Stone."

"Fairy godmothers of the Pax Lineage have the wind," Queen Mangi said, "but you must learn to harness it. It is usually necessary for a girl to master the OneTwoOne Dance, in ballet terms the *pas de deux*, before she has the skills to perform the One

Dance, and the One Dance cannot be mastered until she learns to harness the wind."

"That's a solo, right?"

"The wind is your partner," said Queen Mangi. "You work together as one. Learning these moves also teaches you how to balance the powers of Kalis dance and defense. Give it a try."

"Right now?" I asked. "Here?"

The queen smiled and nodded.

Instinctively, I reached up and moved my arm in an arc, trying to weave strands of the wind that made the fairies fly. My fingers twined around slender filaments of solid air for a glorious moment before the threads disintegrated in a puff.

"Begin like this." Standing on one foot, Queen Mangi demonstrated a series of controlled tai chi–type movements. The results were instant. Bellflowers jingled in the whisper of wind she created with a wave of her hand. A spray of rain arced out of the waterfall with a casual flick of the queen's wrist. Holding her hands palms down as if she were pressing against air lifted her off the floor, like an acrobat pushing against a trapeze bar. "Concentration is the key," she said as she slowly lowered herself.

I closed my eyes, focused on the air around me, and pushed my hands down. I could feel streams of air rush through my fingers, but my feet didn't budge. After three tries, I threw up my hands. I had felt every move Queen Mangi made, and I had been certain I could do it, too, at least a little bit.

"Everyone learns these things in their own time and way, some quickly and some more slowly," Queen Mangi said serenely. "You've ridden the wind more than most girls ever do. Now it is time for you to continue your quest. My fairies cannot hold back the sun much longer."

I wanted to try again, but the queen started walking. "How did you and the reindeer come to be together?" she asked as we headed to the entrance tunnel.

"I saved her from a wolf, and she's been with me ever since." I could see that Ardee was eating from a basket. Several small fairies were scratching her rump and her ears. "She seemed so lost and alone, I wanted to help her. It turns out she helped me just as much as I helped her. And now, well, I just feel somehow connected to her." I realized this was true.

"Still, it is clear she is not your spirikin," the queen said thoughtfully. "I didn't think a reindeer was a fit for you."

I had to ask: "What's a spirikin?"

"Spirikins are unique to the Pax Lineage. No

other fairy godmother has them." Queen Mangi's gaze swept across the cavern. "Spirikins are animal spirits. Each girl's spirikin represents her inner self, and that defines which animal chooses her. The spirikin helps a girl acquire the one quality she needs but doesn't have."

"Oh." I nodded.

"Most spirikins come to girls in the Crystal Cave. Spirikins that choose especially strong-willed girls often decide to fight."

"When do I meet my spirikin?" I asked.

"It will come when you need it most," Queen Mangi said. "So it should be soon. You can't complete your mission until you master your shortcoming."

"What *is* my shortcoming?" I asked.

"You'll figure that out when you meet your spirikin." The queen's gaze turned to a ledge on the wall beside me.

I turned slowly. My breath caught in my throat when I saw the snow leopard staring down at me. The instant the animal caught my eye, it snarled. I had been chosen, and my spirikin wanted to fight.

The queen, Ardee, and the fairies nearby moved out of harm's way as the big cat crouched. An unnatural stillness settled over the cavern.

Then, without so much as a twitch of warning, the snow leopard leapt. I immediately jumped up from the bench and planted my feet. With Kalis stick in hand, I watched the leopard land on the flattened tops of a group of stalagmites. I was no match for the leopard one on one, but I stood my ground despite my pounding heart. I waited for the animal's next move.

The cat waited, too. I wanted to run, but the leopard could catch me in two strides. Taking slow, deep breaths, I checked the terrain on both sides, looking for cover. Before I finished my survey, the cat jumped down.

I bent my knees and launched myself off the floor—but there was nothing within reach to jump onto. As the cat pounced to bring me down, I twisted into a Tornado Spin and barely avoided being smashed by two hundred pounds of snow leopard. My shoulder slammed into a stalactite, and I could feel the cakes in my food pouch go *squash* when I hit the ground. Bruised and breathless, I scrambled between two stalagmites. The cat clawed at my leg and tore my pant leg.

I huddled in the narrow space formed by the crystal towers, staring into the cat's golden eyes. The spirikin sat on its haunches, watching me. A third stalagmite cut off escape to the rear. Overhead, the towers grew so close together, the opening was too small to squeeze through. I had backed into a corner.

The leopard could turn my little Kalis stick into splinters with one bite and claw me to shreds within seconds. I could bite and kick when its teeth clamped on to my boot, but I couldn't win. Staying out of reach was the only way to survive, but I had lost that possibility when I jumped up to nowhere instead of ducking to the side. The cat's gaze only made me more annoyed with myself. I should have taken time to figure out a better strategy!

Rising, the cat backed off a few feet and sat down again, tail flicking back and forth. I barely noticed. Folding my arms on my pulled-up knees, I rested my head and tried to come up with a workable plan. The thought hit me like an electric shock. *That's why the snow leopard had attacked!* It had charged to force me into a fight. It didn't want to harm or eat me. It wanted to test me.

I held the leopard's golden gaze as I crept out of my cramped niche. I rose slowly and, just as slowly, slipped my Kalis stick into my backpack. Dropping my hands to my sides, I faced the snow leopard in surrender. When the leopard crouched, I didn't flinch. When it leapt straight at me, I didn't duck or defend myself. I opened my arms.

We melded into one. Now I *was* the snow leopard. All her instincts and senses were mine. My mother had often said that there was no better teacher than experience.

My mission to reach the summit and find Biba's missing voice was fixed in my leopard mind like prey, and I bolted toward the cavern entrance. My human side felt regret for not bidding the Kalistonia Fairies good-bye, but the feeling fled when my feline focus settled on the reindeer. Big cats and deer are mortal enemies, but the bond between Ardee and me had not been broken by my transformation. As I raced by her, Ardee abandoned the safety of the fairy cavern. She ran after me, and we emerged into the frigid cold outside together.

A predator and loner in the wild, a snow leopard does not have to rely on the reindeer's sensitive nose. I could track our scent back to the path, and although I could talk, I didn't want to use speech any more than necessary.

"What's that?" Ardee's ears perked up at the sound of something stirring in the rocks nearby.

My mouth watered at the scent of rabbit. I remained perfectly still, waiting for the rabbit to show itself. My patience was rewarded when the snow white hare suddenly darted from one mound of rocks to another.

"It's a bunny!" Ardee exclaimed.

I longed to catch it, but I didn't give in to the desire, and the hare scurried into the safety of the rocks. The pull of my human quest was stronger than my new leopard instincts.

Catching Ardee's eye, I made a purring sound in my throat and then headed up the mountain trail. The trek was as easy for me now as it had been hard for me in human form. My thick fur coat kept me warm in the below-freezing temperatures, and my clawed paws didn't slip on the ice and snow. I loped up the path until I caught the scent of wolf.

Stopping beside me, Ardee stared down the trail. There was nowhere to run on the rocky slope, and no place to hide. On her own, she would have been defenseless. But Ardee wasn't alone.

"Go first," I growled.

As the reindeer walked ahead of me, I crouched to scan the snow-covered terrain. I could sense the wolf was coming closer, but I couldn't see it, not even with my feline night vision. The reindeer and I had the advantage of the high ground, and I wanted to make sure we kept it.

"Quickly!" I said.

We pressed onward, digging into the ice and plowing through snowdrifts until we reached a flat area near the top of the mountain. The plateau was the size of a backyard, and it was as high as we could go. The Dayling Mountain's peak rose above us, draped in the golden aura that encircled the distant peaks of Hourling and Yearling, too.

Biba's voice was here to find, but I didn't know where to look. A hint of gray outlined the towers of jagged rock that bordered the plateau on two sides. With the sun rising and time growing short, I padded around the edge of the flat area, peering into crevices and testing for a telltale scent. The last side dropped off into an abyss. I stayed back from the edge. I had used up Queen Patchouli's knots of magic wind, and I couldn't reach the rope pouch anyway. The pouches, my clothes, my backpack, and my Kalis stick had all been absorbed in my blending with my spirikin.

I stood quietly, looking into the night, listening. There was no trace of Biba's voice: not a whimper, a whisper, or a hide-and-seek giggle. There was only the hushed stillness of a winter dawn on top of a mountain.

The reindeer paced back and forth along one of the rock walls, as far from the cliff as she could get. I recognized her actions. A moving target was harder to hit, and she wouldn't accidentally jump off the cliff if something startled her.

Like that wolf, I thought when I saw it glowering at me from a ledge.

Ardee darted to the opposite side of the plateau and stood with her back to the wall. Speed wouldn't help her in this confined area, but if the wolf charged and got past me, she might be able to toss him aside with her antlers. It was the only chance she had if I failed.

But I couldn't fail. Despite Ardee's appetite and her questions, I loved her. Even in the moment, I was startled by the thought. My hackles bristled when the wolf looked at Ardee, and I snarled to get its attention. As I stared into its eyes, my cat-self said to wait, so I did.

The wolf had less patience. Head down and teeth bared, it leapt off the ledge. I side-stepped with a casual calm, as though my opponent were nothing but a pesky puppy. The wolf landed on the ice with legs splayed. Helpless to control an undignified slide, it scrambled to regain its footing and faced me with even greater hostility. The wolf growled and I roared, both of us showing our fangs as we slowly circled each other. I was in no hurry to escalate the contest, but the wolf charged. I jumped clear and batted its ears as it sped by. Furious, the wolf spun around, crouched to spring again, and snarled as it held my feline stare.

Behind the wolf, Ardee was hugging the rocks. The wolf and I stood between her and the path that led down the mountain. As the wolf began to circle me, I pivoted, watching and waiting for the next attack. When it surged toward me, I was ready. But I wasn't prepared for the wolf to suddenly veer toward the reindeer.

"Kerka!" Ardee screamed and lowered her head, aiming her antlers to meet the wolf's charge.

I summoned every ounce of my power and sprang. I landed on the wolf just before it reached Ardee. I clamped my jaws on the thick fur and loose skin at the back of its neck. The wolf twisted underneath me. Losing my grip, I shook fur out of my mouth as the wolf and I rolled, a furious tangle of snapping jaws, slashing claws, and flying fur. I kept fighting until we smashed into the rocks that ringed the arena. The jolt rattled both of us, and we jumped clear.

As we waited, panting and glaring at each other, I realized the leopard wasn't fighting the wolf to the death. The two predators never hunted each other as food in the wild, and they rarely challenged each other over territory. When they did fight, the conflict only lasted until one surrendered and ran away. Even now, my human and cat parts were equally committed to protecting the reindeer and not harming the wolf—if it could be avoided.

The wolf seemed just as determined to have Ardee for dinner. Its lip curled as it stole a glance at the cornered reindeer, and I swiped its nose with my paw. The wolf took a step toward me, and I took a step back, hoping to draw it away. Heading downhill, Ardee could outrun the wolf to the fairy caves. The wolf slowly advanced on me. I continued to back up, and the space between the wolf and the rocks widened.

But Ardee didn't bolt for the trail. She watched me instead, her eyes widening with fear.

Then the wolf suddenly stopped.

I stopped, too, remembering the first time Ardee and I had seen the wolf near a cliff. It had seemed anxious then, almost as though it was afraid of heights.

Sensing an advantage, I took another step back. There was nothing I could do when I heard a sharp crack and the footing crumbled under my hind paws. I threw myself forward and dug into the snow with my front claws, but I couldn't stop my backward slide off the cliff.

"Kerka! Don't leave me!" Ardee screamed as I fell.

A deep sadness filled me as I tumbled into darkness and death. I had failed. I looked up. The summit of Dayling Mountain stood out in stark contrast to the gray light of dawn behind it. The golden aura of the crown was beginning to fade. The wolf had not ventured to the edge of the dropoff, but the reindeer was looking down into the abyss.

"Kerka!" Ardee screamed again. Then she dove off the cliff.

"No!" I shouted back. Everything happened in a split second, but it unfolded before me in slow motion. With her front legs outstretched, the reindeer sliced through the air like an arrow, gaining speed as she fell. I roared with the pain of loss as Ardee plunged by me.

Except that dying was not Ardee's plan. "I'm coming, Kerka!"

I turned my head just as the reindeer pulled out of her dive and flew in a wide arc, heading back in my direction. Astonished, I realized that her ability must have always been there, lying dormant within. This was Aventurine, where, apparently, all reindeer can fly if they want to.

"Get ready!" Ardee rushed toward me, running on air.

When I realized what she had in mind, I hoped everything I had heard about falling cats was true. Using the feline version of a Kalis dance step, I twisted so I was upright, with my legs hanging down. Ardee swooped down and came up underneath me.

I straddled the reindeer's back. Ardee flew in a long, wide arc, so that we rose gradually. She was taking me to the summit. I stayed on, but the extra distance and effort was tiring the reindeer. She faltered as we neared the top, and I slid off her back into the snow the instant we cleared the edge.

But Ardee didn't come in for a soft landing. She fell, and the force cracked the thin rock underneath her. The cliff gave way. As she started to fall, she cried, "I'm too tired to fly!"

That's when the wolf jumped . . . to the rescue.

Clamping its powerful jaws on Ardee's antlers, it planted its feet and pulled. I grabbed the wolf's tail and dug into the ice with my claws, acting as an anchor so the wolf wouldn't go into the abyss, too. The wolf held on, snorting as it tugged and pulled. As soon as the reindeer's front hooves were visible, I began to back up. The wolf and I dragged Ardee to solid ground, where we all collapsed in a heap.

Out of breath and amazed to be alive, I closed my eyes. Every muscle hurt, and I felt the bite of freezing cold in the same instant I heard the joyous shriek of giddy laughter. When my eyes snapped open, I thought I was dreaming within my Aventurine dream.

Biba and Rona were staring down at me, grinning.

And I couldn't stop crying.

Part Three

Zephyr

11

The Secret of the Dance

I shielded my eyes from the sun while it rose over the mountain, and I stared at Biba and Rona as the tears poured down my face. My sisters put their arms around me and held me, saying nothing, just holding me close until finally the tears stopped. I hadn't cried like that when Aiti died. I had barely cried at all.

"I don't know what is the matter with me," I said with a gulp. Then I hugged Biba and Rona both tightly. "How did you get here?" I asked.

"I'm not sure." Rona was dressed for rehearsal in tights, leg warmers, and a turtleneck. She also wore a gray furry vest that looked like the wolf's thick coat. She held her green Kalis stick. "I was waiting at the theater and thinking about wolves when I must have fallen asleep. I had my Kalis stick in my bag. It was the first time I had looked at it in months and I just wanted it near me. Then I dreamed that I was chasing you up a mountain."

"Why were you chasing me?" Since Rona the wolf had been so scary, I was curious.

Rona shrugged. "I don't know why. I just knew I had to catch you, and you kept leaving me behind on purpose, and that made me really mad."

"Are you still mad?" I asked.

"Absolutely not!" Rona glanced down at Biba. "I almost lost both of you. When you went over the cliff, I realized that being so angry was pointless. It couldn't bring Mom back, and it was driving away the other people I love."

Everything happens for a reason in Aventurine, even though the reasons are often mystifying.

"I fell asleep with my Kalis stick last night, too. And I have new boots!" My little sister pulled up her pajama legs to show us her feet. She was wearing furry boots, which were clearly a gift from her reindeer spirikin. Biba was wearing heavy flannel pajamas, and she had her blue Kalis stick in one hand.

"You're talking!" I exclaimed, breaking into a wide grin. I had not failed after all! Biba had her voice back!

"I've been talking," Biba said, planting her

hands on her hips in childish indignation, "ever since you heard me in the woods."

Heard me? The meaning of her words hit me. Biba had been inconsolable when our mother died. She had tried talking to me, and probably to Rona. But Rona had been so angry, she stayed in her room or stayed away from home: she left. And I had been too sad; I couldn't—*wouldn't*—listen because I didn't want to talk about it. Instead, I threw *my*self into school and soccer. Biba had cried out in the only way she thought we might hear her: silently.

And I had found her voice as soon as I had met her as a reindeer. But what had I been missing?

Then I knew what I had been missing and what Biba's voice had helped me find: my heart. Biba had appeared as a reindeer because I somehow felt safer feeling things for an animal. So I could acknowledge my love for her—and that was helping me feel my love, and my sadness, for other things. That's why I had been crying, and crying so hard: they were all the tears I hadn't been able to let out. I realized that now I felt lighter, as if some literal burden had been lifted. People talk about feeling that way, and I had never understood. Now I did. I felt as free as the wind.

"Did you know that reindeers itch?" Biba asked

as she frowned and scratched her neck.

I laughed. "No, I think that's the one thing you didn't complain about."

I couldn't stop shivering. I wasn't wearing my coat when I melded with the snow leopard. It was still on the floor of the fairy cave, where I had dropped it when the furnace creatures blasted me with hot air.

"I think this is yours, Kerka." Rona picked up a golden-white fur cape with black spots and placed it on my shoulders.

"Thanks." I snuggled into the warm fur. Then I had an idea. I slipped off the cape, folded it, and set it on a rock. I pulled my Kalis stick out of my pack and jumped straight up, spinning.

"You've been practicing!" Rona exclaimed, then copied my move. Rona's posture and arm positions were perfect. We jumped and spun several times, and then she called out, "Stroking the Water Horse's Mane!"

Rona and I both switched to the ballerina pose.

Biba was having too much fun twirling in lop-sided circles to join us. It was the first time she had tried a Kalis step since Aiti had died, and she was so caught up in the moment, she forgot why she had ever stopped dancing. "Watch me, Mommy, watch—"

Shocked by her own words and the terrible truth, Biba wobbled to a halt. Her small shoulders shook as she started to cry.

Rona and I rushed to comfort her. "It's okay, Biba." Rona spoke in hushed tones and wrapped her arms around our little sister. "We're here now."

I was too choked up to talk. I touched Biba's short blond braids, wishing there was something I could do to soothe the ache in all our hearts.

"Are those tears?" a familiar voice asked.

I looked up and blinked in disbelief.

"Aiti!" Biba ran toward the rocks where Aiti waited with open arms.

At first I thought the sight of my beautiful mother, with her crown of braided hair, flowing blue gown, and warm smile, was just a vision. Then my mother embraced Biba, and I could see she was real.

Rona and I both ran and threw ourselves into the hug.

"I am happy to see you seeking balance together," my mother said, humor in her voice.

"How can you be here?" Rona asked.

"Aventurine is open to all fairy godmothers when they have something very special or very important to do," Aiti answered.

"Like when you came to get our Kalis sticks," I said. "Right?"

"She wasn't . . . dead then," Rona whispered in my ear so Biba wouldn't hear.

"It's fairy magic," I whispered back. "She's here and she's real. Just be glad."

"I have come to teach you the last basic Kalis step," Aiti said. "Climbing the Sky captures the essence of the wind, and you must learn it before you can master the One Dance."

"The what?" Rona asked, puzzled.

"All things in their proper order," Aiti said. "First let's review all the other steps."

Biba, Rona, and I stood in a line, just as we had for our first Kalis lesson last year, back home. Following our mother's lead, we held our sticks at arm's length and moved them back and forth as we peeked from behind the high grass. With no word spoken, we all flicked our sticks outward.

"Excellent!" Aiti exclaimed. "You're dancing a *pas de trois*! A Dance of Three!"

"Ballet has no such thing!" Rona playfully objected as she continued to perform the reed step.

"This is Kalis," my mother said. "You're sisters with the ability to intuit each other's moves as a trio. Each of you knew exactly when the other two would make the change. When you are skilled, the power of your combined Kalis moves will help our world in a way no other Pax fairy godmothers have been able to for the last few generations."

"What do you mean?" Rona asked.

"You are the first generation with three sisters who look like they will all become fairy godmothers," Aiti explained. "Several hundred years ago, there was a family of six fairy godmother sisters. They accomplished a great deal together, but that is another story." She waved her hand. "So, show me what you have been practicing."

I tried a more advanced test of our skills. Giving no signal, I leapt forward. Rona saw the slight flexing of my knees and read the subtle cue. She performed the jump with me. Biba was a little behind, but she caught up when we added a Tornado Spin.

"Now me!" Biba shifted into the Stroking the Water Horse's Mane stance, holding her left arm out and sliding her stick through the air in elegant loops.

Rona and I spaced ourselves so our swooping sticks wouldn't clash. Aiti leapt into position to the right of Rona. We continued stroking the water horse's mane until our mother launched into another series of Wind Leaps. Rona and I were in nearly perfect sync with her. Biba almost lost her balance, but she just giggled and kept going.

"And now Three Flowers Unfold to meet a new day, one after the other," Aiti said, backing off to give us room. She assumed an at-rest pose and watched as each of us danced the X Sweep, beginning with Rona.

I gloried in my older sister's dazzling precision as I rounded into a ball, held the position, and then sprang from the floor, flinging my arms and legs open like the petals of a flower. I didn't perform with Rona's graceful ease, but I knew I was good in my own way. As I prepared for the final element, I remembered how the Kalistonia Fairy had drifted upward, like a dandelion seed in the step Aunt Tuula called a Zephyr. When I tried it, I felt a gentle push. The boost was ever so slight, and I wanted to ride the wind so much, I assumed I had imagined the assist.

After Biba completed her X Sweep, I saw Aiti's face glow with approval. "Your dancing was most magnificent, Biba, especially since you did not practice ballet or Kalis as Rona and Kerka have the past few months."

Biba grinned with pride.

I was elated. Our mother had been watching over us!

Rona's smile faded when Aiti caught and held her gaze. "I'm so pleased and happy for you, Rona," our mother said. "You've worked hard to become a rising star of ballet in New York, and I'm thrilled with your triumph."

"You're not upset I stopped practicing Kalis?" Rona asked.

"But you haven't quit!" Aiti exclaimed. "You just performed all the steps beautifully. You'll learn everything else you need to know when the time is right for you."

"Kerka made me ride a scary wind," Biba announced.

"I know she did," Aiti said. "Kerka had three magic wind knots, and she used them all wisely." My mother stepped over and touched my cheek. "And that's why I am here now, in Aventurine. Thank you, Kerka."

Crystal bells chimed and a Kalis stick whirred as Queen Mangi appeared in a burst of light. The fairy queen twirled her golden-white stick around her head, flicked her wrist, and telescoped the long stick down. Then she bowed a welcome to my mother, a warm smile on her face.

"How good to see you again, Queen Mangi," Aiti said, bowing back. "You're just in time to watch our final lesson."

"Continue." Grabbing a handful of wind, Queen Mangi rose six feet up onto a small ledge. She tapped the rock with her Kalis stick, and a large toadstool appeared in another flash of light.

Our mother snapped her Kalis stick to get our attention. Instantly, our eyes and ears were fastened on her every move and word.

"The final step in basic Kalis is the hardest, but it unlocks the power we need." Aiti raised her right arm and moved her hand in a circular motion, as though she was twining a rope around her arm. "When you learn to Climb the Sky, you learn to command the wind. And when you command the wind, you can fly."

Everything except my mother disappeared into the background as I watched her demonstrate all the variations of the magical step. Soon my sisters and I were repeating the moves so we wouldn't forget. We reached up with our right hand, then with our left, going through the motions of grasping air that just slipped through our fingers.

"Reach for it!" Aiti rocked forward on her right foot and extended her left leg back, then returned to the starting position. The move reminded me of swinging on a vine. "Feel it!"

As we practiced the new step over and over, I held on to my memory of the ribbon wind and pictured bits of air compressing in my hand.

"Air is a primal element," my mother explained. "It can be molded by a disciplined mind."

I remembered being too cold and tired to continue up the mountain. Yet I had made my legs move with a determined unwillingness to give up. I focused all my passion and willpower: I *would* create a rope that was made of wind.

My hands circled through the air, over and over, first the right and then the left. When my arms began to tire, I ignored my muscles and closed my eyes to concentrate harder. Microscopic bits of air compacted into thin, solid strands against my skin. I pictured the small strands twisting together into larger strands that became a thick rope. When my hand closed around it, I sprang from the ground and whipped my Kalis stick toward the sky. The wind rope pulled me off the ground and carried me up the face of Dayling Mountain.

"Kerka!" Biba yelled. "You're flying!"

The wind roared in my ears and skimmed over my face. My clothes flapped in the crosscurrents. I was airborne, holding on to a wind rope that was lifting me up the side of Dayling Mountain. At first, I didn't open my eyes for fear I'd lose my concentration and fall. This wasn't the same as riding the Redbird Wind with Birdie, and it wasn't like the wind that had come with the knotted rope. I wasn't flying like a bird or being carried. I was riding the wind.

The wind rope was firmly in my grip, and riding it felt as natural as breathing. I wanted the rope to carry me up, but I could also make it take me out or down. Empowered by a confidence that came from deep within, I had become one with the wind.

My gaze was first drawn to the top of the mountain, which was no longer hidden by its golden aura. Beside me, ridges and outcroppings of rock became streaks as I sped by. Directly below, my mother, sisters, and Queen Mangi looked like tiny dolls, growing smaller and smaller against the white snow. The blue sky was laced with cloud tendrils that faded into mist on the horizon all around. I could see the path I had taken from the beach, through the forest, across the meadow and glacier, up the icefall, and over the snow bridge to the fairy caves. The rest of Aventurine was shrouded in mist, a mystery I wouldn't unlock today. It waited, like a present wrapped in cloud paper and tied with a sunbeam, to test other girls from other lineages.

I climbed the sky, going higher and higher. As I rose to the top, I pulled on the wind rope to slow down and reached out with my Kalis stick to touch the high point on Dayling's crown. A rush of joy overwhelmed me as golden mist seeping from the rock suddenly jetted out in streams. Moving my Kalis stick in a wide arc, I circled the summit of the middle queen and pulled the mist with me. Within a few minutes, the golden crown on the Three Queens had been restored.

I began a slow, spiraling descent around the mountaintop. I flew lazily, relishing the wind on my face and the pure freedom of flight. Finally I landed softly between my mother and Queen Mangi.

A humming sound filled the air around me when my feet touched the ground, and a rapid vibration warmed the palm of my hand. My Kalis stick glowed brightly and grew three inches longer.

"What happened to Kerka's stick?" Rona asked.

"The power of a Pax Lineage fairy godmother and her Kalis stick grows with each achievement," Queen Mangi explained. "As will yours someday, maybe soon."

My mother put her arm around my shoulders and held me close. Her smell and her kiss on my hair brought a hundred memories flooding back. I didn't want to leave the safety and warmth of her arms, but she released me when Queen Mangi spoke again.

"Rona and Biba have passed the basic Kalis test as well," Queen Mangi said. "Now each of you may, as you wish and dream, return to Aventurine to continue your fairy godmother training."

"Will Rona and Biba have to climb the Yearling and Hourling mountains to get to the fairy caves?" I asked.

Biba's expression darkened in protest. "I already climbed a mountain!"

"Yes, you did." Queen Mangi laughed. "And now that your generation is whole again, you will enter Aventurine through the Kalistonia Fairies' domain." She paused, then added, "Unless Queen Patchouli summons you into someone else's dream."

That prompted my next question. "Will I ever see Queen Patchouli again?"

My mother answered. "Anything is possible, but no one knows what the future holds, here or in the waking world."

Rona nibbled her lip so she wouldn't cry when she took our mother's hand. "This is our last good-bye, isn't it?"

"No!" Biba threw her arms around our mother's

waist and sobbed into her blue gown.

"It will be okay, Biba." Aiti smiled to reassure us. "In time, the pain will go away, and the memories will make you happy again. Memories are the one gift we have to pass on. I'll always be in your heart, but my time here has passed, and my work is done. You have your father and Aunt Tuula, and now you have your sisters, too. And you all have my love."

Sensing that the sorrowful moment of her departure was upon us, Rona and I pulled Biba away. We held each other as our mother twinkled out like a star.

I couldn't keep back my tears now. I cried on Rona's shoulder, and she cried on mine. Biba buried her face against me and sobbed.

"She's really gone," Rona said. "I'll never stop missing her."

"Neither will I." I wiped the tears off my cheek.

Biba sniffled. "What if I forget her?"

"You won't," Rona said.

"We won't let you." I smiled.

Queen Mangi put her arms around all of us. "Embracing your roles as fairy-godmothers-in-the-making honors your mother every day, no matter where you are. She has passed on the Pax Lineage, and she is part of us as well as you." She kissed the top of each of our heads, then stepped away and disappeared in a burst of light.

"I wish I could do that," said Rona. "Now how are *we* going to get home?"

"I don't want to walk." Biba folded her arms and shook her head.

"I don't want to stay here!" a squeaky voice called out.

Biba ducked behind Rona, and Rona peered at the rocks. "Who's there?"

"It's just me." An elf trudged out of a crevice, holding his green cap in his hands.

"It's an elf," I said.

"But what's he doing here?" Rona's eyes narrowed with suspicion.

"Waiting for you silly girls to go home!" the elf yelled in reply. He wore similar elfin clothes to his brothers, green and red with white fur trim and black boots, but he had his own distinct personality. The beach elf was a joker, and the icefall elf was a grump. This little guy just looked unhappy.

"Why do you want us to leave?" Biba peeked out from behind Rona.

"So I can go home!" He waved his cap in frustration. "My brothers and I can't leave until you do."

I remembered what Aunt Tuula had told me. It was possible—but unproven—that the destinies of Pax Lineage families and elves were intertwined. "Are you and your brothers affected by everything my sisters and I do?"

"Yes!" He rolled his eyes. "I live on Yearling, and the elf in the ice lives on Hourling. We were yanked away when you three stopped talking to each other, and we're stuck here until you patch things up. But it's taken you *forever*!"

"We're back together now," Rona said. "So leave. What's stopping you?"

"I need my message." The stubborn little man scowled and tapped his foot.

I looked him in the eye. "I'll give you the message after you tell us how to get home."

The elf stamped his foot in a brief display of temper. Then, resigned to being outsmarted, he pointed at me. "You have the power. Now deliver the message."

I hesitated, wondering if I had understood him correctly. I decided his words could only mean one thing, so I gave him the message. "Your brother told me to tell you, 'If the wind goes free, so will we.'"

"Finally!" He left in a flash of green and red, moving too fast for my human eyes to follow him. I thought I heard the faraway sound of his brothers laughing.

"What power did he mean, Kerka?" Rona leaned forward to peek over the edge of the drop-off and stepped back.

"It has to be the power of the wind," I said. "We can fly off the mountain. We'll either land somewhere in Aventurine or we'll wake up."

"Are we going to ride the wind again?" Biba jumped up and down and clasped her hands. "Please, please, please."

I raised an eyebrow. "You said you never wanted to ride the wind again, ever."

"That was before I flew to catch you," Biba said, holding out her hand. "It's not scary at all. It's fun!"

Rona didn't look convinced, but she trusted me. "I hope you know what you're doing," she said when she took Biba's other hand.

"Me too!" I laughed as I swept my Kalis stick across the sky. The ribbon wind wrapped itself around us, and we sailed off Dayling Mountain into the morning sky.

Epilogue

I woke up on the sofa in Aunt Tuula's living room. She had left a lamp turned on, and I stared at the ceiling, remembering swooping through the air. Rona and Biba had laughed when we glided past an eagle's nest where a mother bird was feeding her young. My sisters had shrieked in protest when I flew under a stone bridge, and they tensed when we skimmed the ground. Biba and Rona had disappeared while we were circling a meadow of wildflowers—and then I woke up.

Throwing off the blanket, I reached for my Kalis stick. It was under the throw pillow, where I had left it. It looked longer, but I wanted to be sure. I was still wearing socks, and they made no noise on the hardwood floor as I ran.

I turned the light on in my bedroom. My

backpack and the spotted white fur cape were on my bed, as if the fairies had brought them separately. My backpack felt heavy when I went to hang it on the proper hook in my closet. I looked inside, hoping the fairies had left me some water pods. But it was just my schoolbooks. I folded the faux snow leopard cape and put it in a drawer. Then I found a ruler in my desk drawer and held it up to my Kalis stick. It measured fifteen inches, three inches longer than it had measured when I fell asleep.

I slipped my Kalis stick under my pillow and glanced at the clock as I climbed into bed.

It was 2:07 a.m. Saturday. I was thirteen and a true fairy-godmother-in-the-making.

I woke up again around eight and changed out of my sweater and jeans into a turtleneck and comfy sweats. Grabbing my Kalis stick, I leapt out my bedroom door and spun in circles down the hall. I stopped by the container of rain sticks and waved my Kalis stick at the wind chimes across the room. The tinkling ring was drowned out by the clang of pots in the kitchen, and I heard Rona laugh.

"Then Biba puffed up and said, 'I already climbed *this* mountain!'" Rona mimicked Biba's voice.

"Biba talked back to Queen Mangi?" Aunt Tuula chuckled. "The Kalistonia Fairies will have their hands full with our little one, won't they?"

"Actually, I think Queen Mangi liked Biba's attitude," Rona said. "I hope my dreams take me to Aventurine soon. I can't wait to see the fairy caves."

"What was it like being a wolf?" Aunt Tuula asked.

"Awesome," Rona said. "I learned everything I need to know for our production of *Peter and the Wolf*. They don't usually cast a girl to dance the wolf, you know."

"I know," Aunt Tuula said.

I hurried into the kitchen to join them. Rona was seated at the island, and Aunt Tuula was cooking. "There's the birthday girl!" Aunt Tuula's face was smudged with flour. "We're having blueberry pancakes with strawberry syrup and sweet sausages."

"Sounds wonderful," I said as I hopped up on the stool beside Rona. "I'm famished."

"I'm not surprised, after all that gallivanting around Aventurine," Aunt Tuula said, spooning pancake batter onto a hot griddle. "Did you have fun?"

"It was fun and cold and scary and so much happened I don't know where to start." I put my Kalis stick down and took a tangerine out of a bowl.

"You have all weekend to tell me." Aunt Tuula poured tea into a cup and handed it to me. "Right now, we have some other very serious business to take care of."

My hand froze on the sugar spoon. Serious usually meant trouble. "What?"

"Birthday presents!" Aunt Tuula reached under the counter and pulled out a box wrapped in lavender paper with a bright red bow. "I'm baking a cherry-chocolate cake later, but you don't have to wait. You can open it now."

I finished adding sugar and cream to my tea. Then, ever so carefully, I slipped off the red ribbon and peeled away the tape.

"It's just paper, Kerka!" Rona teased. "Hurry up. The suspense is awful."

"Okay, okay." I liked to make the suspense last, but it was so nice to have my sister back, I ripped the paper. Aunt Tuula's gift was an enameled box with an image of the fairy cave on the lid. "Oh, Aunt Tuula! It's beautiful."

"It's a keepsake box, but there's more. Look inside." Aunt Tuula quickly flipped the pancakes, then turned back to watch as I raised the hinged lid.

What looked like a pile of wood and metal rested on the green felt that lined the inside of the box. I hooked my finger on a metal ring and lifted it up. The ring was part of a chain that was attached to a thatched canopy. A ceramic elf dressed exactly like the Dayling beach brother stood on a circle of wood under the thatched roof. Silver tubes dangled from the circle.

"It's an elf wind chime!" I exclaimed. "I love it!"

"When I saw it in the shop window I couldn't resist." Aunt Tuula beamed. "Something told me that was *your* elf. I didn't expect you to find out that Pax Lineage families and elves really are connected."

"We are, but I can't prove it," I pointed out.

"I believe you." Aunt Tuula scooped the pancakes off the griddle, putting two on each plate.

"I have something for you, too." Rona handed me a card and watched while I opened the flap. There were three tickets inside.

"Are these for the opening night of your ballet?" I asked, hoping I looked as pleased as I felt.

"For you, Aunt Tuula, and a friend," Rona said. "Maybe Birdie Bright would like to go. Those aren't ordinary tickets. They're backstage passes."

"Super!" I threw my arms around Rona's neck and hugged her. "I bet you'll be the best wolf ever."

Aunt Tuula added two sausages to the pancakes and set the breakfast plates in front of us. After a playful tussle over the syrup, Rona and I took turns talking between bites. By the time we finished eating, we had covered all the high points of our adventure.

"Well, you girls are certainly off to a good start with your fairy godmother training." Aunt Tuula poured more tea.

"There's a whole lot more to being a good fairy godmother than I realized," Rona said.

"I'll say!" I reached for another tangerine.

When the phone rang, Aunt Tuula answered it. She listened a moment, then held the receiver out to me. "It's your father, Kerka."

I set my half-peeled tangerine aside and wiped the juice off my fingers with a napkin. My hand shook a little when I took the phone. As much as I loved Aunt Tuula and New York, I missed the rest of my family back in Finland. "Hi, Dad!"

He wished me a happy birthday and asked how I was doing. He sounded happier, as though the weight of sadness and worry had been lifted off him, too. After he gave me a quick report on my old soccer team, he said, "I have a surprise for you."

There were some muffled thumps, then—

"Hi, snow leopard," Biba said in Finnish.

"I'm so happy to hear your voice, Biba!" I said, a huge smile on my face. I was also happy that Biba remembered our Aventurine journey. "How are you?"

"I'm hungry!" Biba laughed.

"You're *always* hungry!" I joked, laughing with her.

The rest of the weekend alternated between Kalis dancing and lazy lounging. Rona was totally committed to mastering the Climb the Sky step, and she wanted my help. As soon as she returned from ballet rehearsal, we practiced until we were too tired to walk. Then we watched a movie; ate some of Aunt Tuula's fantastic cheese, tomato, and cauliflower casserole; slept; and started all over again on Sunday. By Monday morning, I was glad I had to go to school. I couldn't wait to tell Birdie in person about my mission in Aventurine, and my aching muscles needed a rest.

It was still cold in New York, and a brisk breeze blew through the concrete canyons. I loved exhaling frosty breath and hearing the crackling sound of salt and ice under my boots as I walked toward the Girls' International School of Manhattan. I now felt as free on the city streets as I had on the top of Dayling Mountain.

An elderly couple strolled arm in arm ahead of me. I didn't try to pass them on the narrow stretch of sidewalk, but slowed my pace instead. I had plenty of time, and I didn't want to be rude. Besides, I was enjoying the city with the interest of a fairy-godmother-to-be. On this particular morning, as though celebrating my success, all seemed right in the world.

"Oh dear!" the elderly woman cried out when her husband's hat blew off his head. "There goes your favorite cap."

The old man hobbled after the hat, but he couldn't catch it. He stopped at the curb, too breathless to chase the hat into the street.

The hat tumbled down the center of the busy street toward the oncoming traffic. With a wave of my hand, I asked the wind to catch the hat just before a cab rolled over it. Then, snapping like a whip, the wind flipped the hat back toward its owner. The old man grabbed it.

"How did you do that?" his wife asked, amazed.

"Don't know, but I got my cap back." He took her arm again. "And now I'm really ready for bagels and coffee."

My first waking-world good deed was a simple task that had touched only two lives, but the gesture made me feel like a real fairy godmother. It felt good.

• • •

Birdie was waiting for me by the front door of GIS. She was all smiles and bouncing on the balls of her feet. She obviously had something huge that she wanted to tell me. I was sure my stories about Aventurine were bigger and better, but Birdie didn't give me a chance to even say hello. She greeted me with a loud "Happy birthday!" Then she shoved a chocolate cupcake with a pink candle in my face.

"For me?" I took the cupcake and licked the frosting. "Wow. That tastes really good."

"That's just a tease," Birdie said, jiggling with excitement. "You'll never guess who I just found."

I thought about it for a second. "I give up," I said. "Who?"

Birdie gave a wide grin with her braces showing. "Zally the magic mapmaker, that's who!"

Acknowledgments

This book is inspired by my many years as a dancer. So I must thank my earliest dance teachers from when I was nine to sixteen years old, Maxine Asbury and Patsy Swayze of the Greater Houston Civic Ballet Company. I want to also give a nod to my current teacher, Minna of Finland, who is bringing out my "inner" kickboxer and martial artist—a must for perfecting a Kalistonian Zephyr. I give thanks to the children in my life, young and old, who believe in animal spirits and who will howl at a full moon with me. Thanks to Diana Gallagher for her help in realizing my story, including Kerka, the spirikin, and Ardee. The mountain climb was worth it! Thanks to my design and production team in Austin—Mario Champion, Mo Serrao Cole, Lurleen Ladd, Maria Meinert, Anne Woods, Roanna Gillespie, Evan

Bozarth, Dustin Bozarth, Kim Cristiano, Andrea Burden, Cameron Jordan, and Jan Wieringa. It is a blast to work with such talented and dedicated people who believe in this dream and put their souls into the work. And thanks and much love to my son Shane Madden for cowriting and producing the amazing Kalis dance song, "121."

The Aventurine dream continues, thanks to Mallory, Chelsea, and the tireless marketing and sales staff at Random House.

A Memorial Note from the Author

Andrea Burden, the illustrator of *Kerka's Book* and *Birdie's Book*, passed away in December 2009. She left behind two daughters, Bella and Indira. Andrea was a consummate mother, daughter, friend, and guide, and was a true fairy godmother to many. She was an artist who brought forth the feminine in everything she did. When I conceived of Kerka's story, I never imagined that its central theme involving the loss of a mother would hit so close to home. Andrea will be loved forever through her art and her daughters and these books.

About the Author

Jan Bozarth was raised in an international family in Texas in the sixties, the daughter of a Cuban mother and a Welsh father. She danced in a ballet company at eleven, started a dream journal at thirteen, joined a surf club at sixteen, studied flower essences at eighteen, and went on to study music, art, and poetry in college. As a girl, she dreamed of a life that would weave these different interests together. Her dream came true when she grew up and had a big family and a music and writing career. Jan is now a grandmother and writes stories and songs for young people. She often works with her own grown-up children, who are musicians and artists in Austin, Texas. (Sometimes Jan is even the fairy godmother who encourages them to believe in their dreams!) Jan credits her own mother, Dora, with handing down her wisdom: Dream big and never give up.

Don't miss

Zally's Book

Coming soon!

Turn the page for a preview.

(Dear Reader, please note that the following excerpt
may change for the actual printing of *Zally's Book*.)

From Zally's Book

From between a couple of willows, I saw a lady coming toward me who was cooler than any fairy-tale princess. She was a real fairy. Not the tiny you-can-hit-it-with-a-flyswatter type of fairy, but a tall, elegant lady with delicate, iridescent blue wings that opened and closed like a butterfly's. Flowers twined through her crown, which seemed to be made of dewdrops that had frozen into diamonds. Her hair was longer than mine, flowing to her knees, and she wore a beautiful, fluttery gown of the palest lilac. The scent of lilacs hung about her as well. A cascade of miniature silver bells on her earrings made a faint tinkly sound when she moved her head. She stopped a few feet away from me and, in a solemn voice, said, "Welcome, Zally."

How did she know my name? That's when I

knew it: I was dreaming. Still, I wanted to be polite. So I gave a small curtsy and said, "Thank you . . . Your Majesty?"

She smiled. "You may call me Queen Patchouli. Come with me, Zally." She waved a dainty hand toward the trees. "We should get started right away. Do you have any questions?"

Questions? Of course I had questions! About a million, in fact. But instead of asking any of them, I blurted, "Why—I'm just asleep, right? What do I need to know about my dreams?"

She tilted her head and looked at me. "You may be sleeping in your own world, but you are awake here. And this is no ordinary dream. This is Aventurine. You could spend days or even weeks here while you're asleep in your own world. But you don't need to worry about how long you stay in Aventurine. You'll wake up in your own bed, and only one night will have passed."

My mouth fell open. "Did you say Aventurine? It—it's real?" I followed Queen Patchouli down to the rocky stream, and we began to walk along it. The grass tickled my bare feet. "No, Aventurine can't be real. I would know. It's not on any map."

"Not yet," she agreed. "But wouldn't you like it to be?"

I would love to see such an amazing place mapped out. I had often wanted to draw Aventurine and hadn't been able to. It would be wonderful to see everything, draw maps of the landscape, have adventures. I thought of another question.

"Are you the queen of all Aventurine?"

As we walked beside the babbling stream, she explained that she was only the queen of the Willowood tribe of fairies, and that there were many more fairy queens throughout the land, each with her own queendom.

"How many fairy godmothers are there?" I asked.

"How many people are in a family?" she asked me in return.

That was a strange response. "How much of the family do you mean? Just my parents and brothers and me? Six. With Abuelita, seven."

The fairy queen said, "That is just *your* family. But how many people are in any family?"

I found the question frustrating. "That depends. Some families are very small. Or should I include cousins and aunts and uncles and grandparents . . . great-grandparents, even? There are lots of ways to count family members, so there's no easy answer."

She nodded. "That's how many fairy godmothers there are."

I tried a different question. "Do I know any other fairy godmothers?"

"You know your mother and grandmother, don't you? You will learn to recognize others."

"How old does a girl have to be to become one?" I asked.

"Most potential fairy godmothers begin their serious training between twelve and fourteen."

Not exactly what I had asked. "How long does fairy-godmother training take?"

"How long does it take someone to become a brilliant musician?" Queen Patchouli countered.

"You know that's not a fair question. Everyone's different." I frowned. "Some people have no interest in becoming musicians, so they don't even try. Some enjoy music but never get really good at it. Others have natural talent and develop quickly. Then there are people who have to work hard for ages until they get to the same point."

"Exactly," said Queen Patchouli.

We walked and talked for what felt like hours. Eventually we passed through a dense grove of trees, then out into a glade. There, flower-bedecked fairies flitted about doing their work—whatever it is that fairies do. At the center of the glade stood a small desk and chair. On the desk was a large leather-bound book the size of an unabridged dictionary. I wondered if it might be an atlas, and hurried forward to take a look.

"This is *The Book of Dreams*, Zally," Queen Patchouli said. "I need you to write your dream in it."

"But I don't usually remember my dreams," I said.

The fairy queen smiled. "You are dreaming right now. And I guarantee that you will remember this dream when you awaken. But that is not the sort of dream that is entered in *The Book of Dreams*. The book is for your hopes and desires, what you would like to do or become. You could just write a hope for today, but far-ranging dreams are often more satisfying for the book. When you are done, we will talk about your quest."

"There's not much to discuss, since I've never been on a quest."

The queen motioned for me to sit at the desk. "Well," she said, "you are about to go on a quest. All the girls from your world who might someday become fairy godmothers come to Aventurine for training, which usually takes the form of a quest. The family talisman of their lineage is often important to their success, and the girls' adventures help them learn how to use the gifts they were born with. Do not be afraid to use the cacao pod, Zally. It will not be harmed."

"Okay." I didn't know what I would use the cacao pod for, but I knew by now that Queen Patchouli wouldn't just tell me what to do. I laid my bag on the table by the book and sat down. "So Mamá and Abuelita sort of went to school here?"

"Yes," the queen said, "as the other women of the Inocentes line did before them. But not every girl who *could* become a fairy godmother *does* become one. Some girls choose a different path. And some . . ."

"They flunk out?" I asked.

She nodded.

I swallowed hard. "I'm a good student. I get straight A's. Don't worry, I won't fail."

"Aventurine does not have the sort of classroom you're used to," she warned. The fairy queen seemed to be choosing her words carefully. "In a sense, the entire land of Aventurine is an academy for teaching fairy godmothers. You are already in the 'classroom.'"

I chuckled. "I guess I should have realized that from the way you made me answer my own questions. Are you my teacher?"

She shook her head. "Many girls who come to Aventurine start here with the Willowood Fairies. But it is when you leave us that your most important learning begins. Everyone and everything you encounter will teach you: the terrain, the creatures, your companions, your adventures. You will choose whom to listen to and how to learn, and in many ways you will be your own teacher. It is like that in the waking world as well—you just have to see it."

I gave her an uncertain look. "Okay, what's my first assignment? Or homework? Or whatever you call it?"

"First you will write something that you very much desire in *The Book of Dreams*. You'll find that writing in Fairen, our language, comes naturally to you—you are speaking it already."

She waved a hand in the air. A snow-white peacock appeared, strutting toward us. The bird fanned out its sparkling tail feathers proudly, nearly blinding me as they caught the sunlight. Through squinted eyes I watched the peacock bow its head to the queen.

Queen Patchouli bowed her head in return. "We need one of your feathers, my beautiful friend," she said.

Turning its back toward us, the peacock shook itself, sending out a shower of light, and released a glittering white feather from its tail. The plume drifted gently to the ground. Murmuring her thanks to the bird, the fairy queen picked up the quill and placed it gently on top of *The Book of Dreams*. She lifted the lid off a small shell bowl that sat near the book. Inside was a silver liquid.

"Your pen," she said, touching the feather. "Your ink." She pointed to the liquid. "Your paper," she said as the pages riffled on their own and the book opened to a blank one.

"What did Mamá and Abuelita write? Can I read their dreams?" I asked.

The fairy queen answered, "They wrote what their hearts told them to write, and you will read it . . . eventually."

With that big book open, full of the dreams of fairy godmothers who came before me, and with the blank page facing me, I felt kind of intimidated. I've written stories and journals, but nothing that was part of a *real* book, a book that would be kept and read by others, a book that, by the looks of it, could be a thousand years old or more.

But one of the reasons I'm a good student is that I've discovered a secret: sometimes when an assignment seems big, scary, or super-important, I just have to start writing—writing anything—and let my mind get buried in the subject. Once I get going, things get clearer, and I wonder why I was worried about it in the first place. So that's what I did in *The Book of Dreams*.

October 25, 2008

I want to travel to different lands, meet new people, see animals I've only heard of. Plus I want to make a map of my travels. Most of all, I want to make a map of Aventurine, because there isn't one. I want to help other girls who need to find their way, by making a map to help them on their travels, too.

Zally Guevera

I closed my eyes and pictured the places I had already seen in Aventurine. Then, dipping the peacock-feather quill back into the silvery ink, I drew a map of the meadow and the willow trees and the babbling stream and the forest and the fairy glade at the bottom of the page. The ink dried instantly, and I was pleased with my work. A moment later, I shook my head in amazement as ornaments surfaced in the margins, coloring in my little map until it looked like a page in one of those illuminated books from the Middle Ages that were painted by hand.

A breeze blew in and ruffled the pages of the book again. It opened to a dream written in Abuelita's handwriting. The magic of *The Book of Dreams* made the words easy for me to read. Abuelita's entry was about wanting to help people, especially innocents, by giving them food and care, and sharing with them the magic of the cacao. I wondered what she meant by that. At the very bottom of the page she had written a recipe. Before I could read it, the wind blew the pages again. There was my mother's handwriting— something about giving children the chance to go to school, and making sure that people had pets to show them love. The pages fluttered, and *The Book of Dreams* closed with a solid thump.

But the little I had been able to see had taught me more than ever how important dreams are.

My desire to map Aventurine was now permanently entered into *The Book of Dreams*. It was there for fairies, and fairy-godmothers-in-training, to read for hundreds or thousands of years to come—almost like being a published author! I was still in a bit of a daze thinking about it, when a new question occurred to me.

"You said that I'm of the Inocentes Lineage of fairy godmothers—women who help innocents. That's not what I wrote about in *The Book of Dreams*, though. What does making maps have to do with helping innocents?" I asked.

Queen Patchouli led me out of the glade and down a path that looked like it was made of crystal shards, though they felt soft against my bare feet.

The fairy queen seemed to consider my question seriously before answering. "Well, you will be helping fairy-godmothers-in-training who come after you to find their way when they go on their quests. It is a special gift that you have. No one has mapped Aventurine before. But mapping is certainly not the only ability you will develop on your quest. Simply by going, you will learn many skills you need for helping innocents."

"Maybe I should know this already, but what exactly *is* an innocent? How can I tell if someone is innocent? Does it have anything to do with doing good things and bad things? Is there some sort of test for who is innocent and who's not?"

Queen Patchouli tilted her head thoughtfully. The tiny bells on her earrings tinkled. "The fairy godmothers of the Inocentes Lineage are not asked to judge who is good and who is evil, so much as they are expected to help those who are in need—especially those who are not capable of helping themselves. Most often, innocents are young children or animals, but some innocents may be old—those who have lost their memories, for example. In your travels you will learn to recognize innocents, and you will be drawn to those who most need your help."

¡Ay, mira! That seemed like a lot to expect of me. I mean, I was just barely thirteen, and I thought working in our bakery was too much responsibility

sometimes. Would I have to become some sort of super Girl Scout or a saint—Mother Teresa, maybe? I couldn't possibly help everyone I met who needed help; I'd never be able to sleep or eat or go to school. Then my mind went to something else the fairy queen had said: *In your travels.*

This couldn't be true. I had always wanted to travel, and now I was going to do it in Aventurine? I pinched myself. It felt real enough to hurt. This was going to be so cool! I felt my worries lessen as my excitement grew.

"We're here. You'd better get ready for your quest now," the fairy queen said, glancing down at my bare feet. She made a swirling motion with one hand, and in front of me a circle of bright green grass sprang up from the ground, like water spraying from a fountain. But instead of falling back down as water would, the ring of grass—almost ten feet high— stayed in place, swaying gently in the faint breeze. From the edge of the grass circle all the way to my feet, a pathway of springy soft moss, dotted with white flowers, grew in just a few seconds.

"Be sure to take that with you," Queen Patchouli said, waving her hand gracefully at my woven Guatemalan bag, which was on the ground beside me. "Everything you need will be in there."

Picking up my bag, I felt for the cacao pod in-side. It was still there. Then I walked down the path and used both hands to separate the stalks of grass at the edge of the circle so I could look inside. The circle was hollow. It formed a tiny roofless room, like a changing room in a store—only alive. I stepped in, admiring the pink, yellow, and lavender wildflowers that carpeted the ground. I saw nothing else in the room. That was strange. Was I supposed to know how this magic worked?

I slipped the woven bag off my shoulder and had reached in to pull out the cacao pod, when some-thing brown and hard sprang out of the opening, startling me. I dropped the bag and backed away. The hard brown thing seemed to be a piece of wood, like a branch or a tree trunk with no leaves, and it shot straight up to the sky and stopped at exactly the same height as the grass of the circle. Then it started to thicken, and it elongated in several directions. Little flaps of wood began unfolding, clattering as they moved. It happened so fast, I can hardly de-scribe it now, but within a minute a huge wooden wardrobe stood before me.

Yes, I said *wardrobe*. The dark wood at the base was carved with figures of lambs and kittens, dogs and squirrels, birds and rabbits. At the top of the wardrobe, the carved face of a child smiled down at me. I was still a bit spooked by my woven bag's jack-in-the-box imitation, so I was very careful when I stepped toward it. Who knew? A whole department store might pop out! Then again, the wardrobe might be filled with fur coats and mothballs, and the back might lead to a mystical land where it was always winter. . . .

As it turned out, neither thing happened. I looked around on the ground for my bag, hoping my family talisman hadn't been squashed by the wardrobe. I didn't see the bag, so I stood to one side and gingerly pulled open one of the wardrobe doors, which had a mirror attached to the inside. Relaxing a bit, I opened the second door. Another mirror. In the wardrobe was a long rod with clothes of every kind and color hanging on it. Below that, there were drawers filled with gloves, belts, hats, and dozens of other accessories. A shelf on top of the drawers displayed all sorts of shoes, boots, sandals, and slippers. And *everything* seemed to be my size!

From outside, the fairy queen said, "Take what you need from the wardrobe now. This will be your only chance to prepare for your journey."

How was I supposed to know what I needed? I looked through the clothes, pulling out different items and holding them up to look at myself in the mirrors. I tried on a pink-and-gold silk sari, a German dirndl in green and red with a white blouse, a Plains Indian dress made of fringed buckskin, a jump-suit of some smooth silvery material that looked like it should be worn by an astronaut, a crinoline petticoat, a beautiful blue kimono with silver-and-orange embroidered goldfish and a lavender obi, a khaki bush-exploration outfit complete with pith helmet, a deep purple cheongsam dress, and more. I found scarves and belts that jingled with little coins, long feather boas, lace mantillas, and peasant blouses.

I finally decided that I should be practical. I chose a pair of brown leggings, a light-as-air pink cotton shirt that had billowy sleeves, and a cropped brown vest that reminded me of Guatemala, with flowers embroidered all over it. Then I pulled on a pair of purple boots that went up to my knees. They were made out of a material I'd never felt before — something between silk and leather.

When I was satisfied with my outfit, I started to tidy up. I picked up an armful of the items I had tried on, but before I could put them back, I heard a whooshing sound. Then a force like the wind yanked the clothes right out of my hands, except for one long silky scarf that seemed to wrap itself around one of my wrists. Moments later, all of the clothing — except for what I was wearing and the scarf—was back in its correct place. Even faster than the wardrobe had assembled itself, it shrank back into my bag and disappeared, like smoke being sucked into a vacuum cleaner.

I lifted my bag, half expecting it to weigh a ton from the wardrobe I had seen go into it, but it felt completely normal. I looked inside. To my relief, the cacao pod was intact. I tucked the scarf, which was the light purple of an early dawn, into the bag and slung it over my shoulder.

Instantly, the circle of grass around me shrank away. In a few seconds the grass was the same height as all the other grass in the area. I could see Queen Patchouli waiting for me.

"What do you think?" I asked, spinning so she could see my outfit.

"I think that you are ready for—"

Just then, a horse and rider galloped up the crushed-crystal path and came to a stop right in front of us in a spray of sparkling gravel. The horse, its coat dark with sweat, was a big golden palomino with four tall white stockings and a flaxen mane and tail. But something caught my eye when the horse shook its neck—the mane was shot through with strands of real gold, which created a metallic sheen that caught the light. The horse wasn't wearing a saddle or a bridle.

Astride the bareback horse was a girl with wild coral-colored hair who looked as though she had been riding for a long time. There were smudges of dirt on her face, and perspiration glistened on her forehead. Miniature shells dangled from her earlobes and hung from a chain around her neck. She looked about my age and height. The girl slumped over the horse's neck and held on, gasping for breath. Then I noticed that on her back was a pair of peach-tinted wings, shimmery and sheer like the wings of the other fairies, except for one thing—one of her wings was broken.

Turning her head toward us, the fairy girl said, "Queen, I come on an urgent errand from Kib Valley. We need your help."

Have you read the first
Fairy Godmother Academy book?

Birdie's
Book

Available now!